Author and illustrator Laura Dockrill is a graduate of the BRIT School of Performing Arts and has appeared at many festival and literary events across the country, including the Edinburgh Fringe, Camp Bestival, Latitude and the Southbank Centre's Imagine Festival. Named one of the top ten literary talents by *The Times* and one of the top twenty hot faces to watch by *ELLE* magazine, she has performed her work on all of the BBC's radio channels, including Gemma Cairney's Radio 1 show, plus appearances on Huw Murray, Colin Murray and Radio 4's *Woman's Hour*. Laura was the Booktrust Online Writer in Residence for the second half of 2013 and was named as a Guardian Culture Professionals Network 'Innovator, Visionary, Pioneer' in November 2013. Laura has been a roving reporter for the Roald Dahl Funny Prize, and is on the advisory panel at the Ministry of Stories. The first *Darcy Burdock* book was shortlisted for the Waterstones Children's Book Prize 2014. She lives in south London with her bearded husband.

The *Darcy Burdock* series is Laura's first writing for children. After having her stage invaded by fifty rampaging kids during a reading of her work for adults at Camp Bestival, she decided she really enjoyed the experience and would very much like it to happen again. Laura would like to make it clear that any resemblance between herself-as-a-child and Darcy is entirely accurate.

'Everyone's falling for Laura Dockrill' – VOGUE

On
Obviously
Darcy
Burdock

by LAURA DOCKRILL

CORGI BOOKS

DARCY BURDOCK: OH OBVIOUSLY
A CORGI BOOK 978 0 552 57254 5

Published in Great Britain by Corgi Books,
an imprint of Random House Children's Publishers UK
A Penguin Random House Company

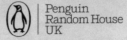

Penguin
Random House
UK

This edition published 2015

1 3 5 7 9 10 8 6 4 2

Typeset in 12.5/17pt Bembo by Falcon Oast Graphic Art Ltd

Corgi Books are published by Random House Children's Publishers UK,
61–63 Uxbridge Road, London W5 5SA

www.**randomhousechildrens**.co.uk
www.**totallyrandombooks**.co.uk
www.**randomhouse**.co.uk

Addresses for companies within The Random House Group Limited can be found at:
www.randomhouse.co.uk/offices.htm

THE RANDOM HOUSE GROUP Limited Reg. No. 954009

A CIP catalogue record for this book is available from the British Library.

Printed and bound by CPI Group (UK) Ltd, Croydon, CR0 4YY

For the Buckles
And for Doll Face

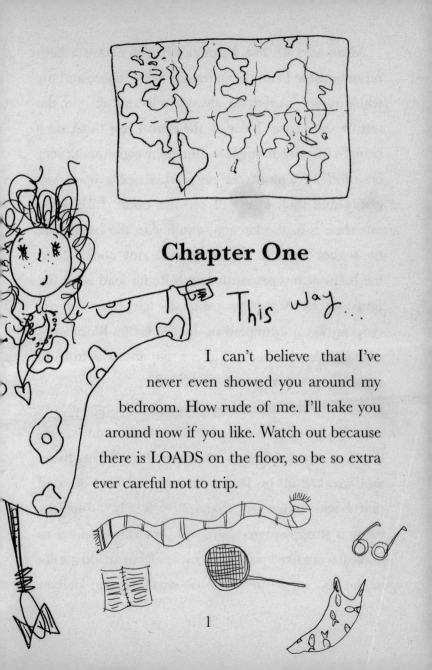

Chapter One

This way...

I can't believe that I've never even showed you around my bedroom. How rude of me. I'll take you around now if you like. Watch out because there is LOADS on the floor, so be so extra ever careful not to trip.

1

Mum says it's like I practically don't have a bed-room because I can't keep myself to one room and my whole entire everything always spills out all over the rest of the house. Most of the time I just think she's being a moany mongoose but then sometimes, very occasionally, a crack in my eyeball splits open *very* gently and then I sort of see her point. Like when one shoe is in the kitchen, another in the bathroom, my school bag is in the living room, my books are in the hallway, my pet lamb Lamb-Beth's lead is on the stairs, my nail varnishes are by the telephone and my crisp packet is crumpled up by the kettle. But it's not my fault that I'm far too interesting and wondrous to waste my precious time CLEANING.

Up the stairs, my bedroom is on the left, opposite my sister Poppy's. We used to have two beds in one room, but then one day I made an anger storm in my brain and wrecked all of Poppy's things and Dad decided that I had 'outgrown' that space. Really, I was just being a stroppy angry little cow, but Dad decided to make it seem like I was not a cow at all but an old gorilla in the zoo whose pen was too small. So the kitchen table became Dad's office and his office became my new room. It's small. But it's all by my own and I love it.

And anyway I HATE zoos.

All over the walls are hundreds of bajillions of pictures of things that I take the time to notice and admire. Things that I enjoy or like. Some of the things are tickets from things I've been to or postcards or birthday cards, some are things that I have cut out and stuck on from like magazines. At first Mum was cross. She said it was 'ruining the walls', but then she gave up caring and let me wallpaper the walls with my interests. It looks like one giant collage. Sometimes I lie there for ages, looking at all the things together, even though I've seen everything a billion and one times. It never gets boring.

The next noticeable thing is obviously my bed. It is a normal one-person bed with two pillows. I have some teddies on my bed.

At school, Clementine, the wretched twit, who happens to be from America, calls all teddies 'stuffed animals'. But I HATE that phrase because it seems as though all teddies are dead and then have been stuffed and THAT just ISN'T true. ONE BIT.

So I still call them *teddies*, even though some of them aren't even teddy bears. At school we all mostly say we don't like teddies any more, but that just also isn't true. I don't like it if in the night I roll over and knock one of my teddies onto the floor. I feel really guilty like they might have a bruise or something. I always kiss it better, but not too much in case there is a secret camera filming my every move, and when I'm thirty and my life is going *really* successful I might go on a TV chat show and they might show clips of me doing stupid things and everybody will see my whole embarrassing moments and me kissing my teddy would probably make it to the final edit. And we can't be having that.

You'll notice the huge drawers that can't quite shut as they are spilling out with clothes of every colour and pattern like multi-coloured alien tongues, flappy pokey little squares of material. The wardrobe doors are always swung open too, with its guts pouring out onto the ground; by guts, I mean coats and shoes and

a tennis racket and hair stuff and towels (whoops, they
are not meant to be in here) and a dressing gown and
a sleeping bag and a feather boa and lots of other
stuff that shouldn't be there at all really. It looks like a

unicorn has vomited a rainbow onto the ground. Have you noticed that when you need *one* thing loads . . . say, like a sleeping bag or a tennis racket, it's one of those things that you can always imagine being everywhere? You know you are SURE that you've seen it, and then in your brain you can picture it everywhere, and that's because it's one of those things that ends up in wardrobes. For one reason or another.

Then there are my books that are meant to be on a shelf but instead . . . this is just them . . . *Oh, hi, we're everywhere.*

Then there's my desk but it's just covered in more clothes and stuff that has nothing to do with a desk unless you count the wonderful map of the world that Dad stuck on the wall in front of it to inspire me. And there's a dictionary. Which I never read, as I far prefer to make words up and create my own language. Obvs.

And on the back of that chair sits one of my most special things, a blanket that I got for Christmas. It's purple and green and fluffy and it looks like a scraggy old witch's cape and I LOVE it, and her name is 'Witchy' and I wrap her round me when I'm feeling cold or not so full of comfort. I think I might want to wrap old Witchy around me right this second because I notice, all crinkled up, rolled into a tiny square, the ink spoiled and wretched: THE INVITE.

THE INVITE

to . . .

the school sleepover.

Everybody else has their invites pinned on their walls, or tucked away in their rucksack front pockets, or even taped to their weekly planners. But not me. Mine is folded into the tiniest square that paper would allow. Why? Because I do NOT want to go.

Why don't I want to go?

Because it will be truly ghastly and here are the reasons.

1.   Sleepovers are meant to be fun. 'School' and 'fun' are not words that like to hang out together. Obviously.

2.   Because there is going to be a 'talent show' and Clementine, the ghastly brute of all eternity, is doing – in her own words – 'a concert'. GROSS.

3.   Because everybody has to wear their best most

fantastic pyjamas, and all my pyjamas come from the land of alien baby world and say far too much about the secretive astonishing side of my personality and will showcase me as an immature rugrat, and I don't fancy being the laughing stock of the entire world. As per usual. AND, because Mum and Dad are poorer than poor at the moment, they are refusing to buy me new normal pyjamas so that I may at least HAVE A GO at fitting in.

I sigh. All deep. Like a parent.

I unfold the square invitation. It's gross. I don't know why I'm taunting myself. You don't have to be the smartest cookie in the cookie jar to see Clementine's wretched graphic design handiwork all over it. Well, I think the oversized image of her singing into a

⊲ VaM!
▽ — BLEUGH!
↖ YUCK!

microphone and dressed as a pop star wannabe wombat also helps give *that* away.

And I can't not go. I wish I could not go, but I know Mum and Dad would do anything to get me out the house for a bit. Plus, it's for charity and plus . . . I can't let Will go without me. All it might take is one evening without my watchful eye upon him for him to immediately spring at the chance to find a new best friend.

I have to suck it up. Like a champion.

I fold the square back up. I'll finish telling you about my room and dread my life until the Friday of the sleepover approaches.

I have a window too. In my room. To just, you know, look out of, or as a portal in case a vampire ever decides to visit. I am sure the vampire will use the window as an entrance.

My door is quite battered because I am a ten out of ten clumsy person, and also I slam my door quite a lot when I'm in a bad mad mood or I want somebody to get out of my room or if I feel like throwing myself on top of my bed and having a good old massive cry. I step out of it now.

On the front, in my own handwriting, on a piece of paper, it says:

> Writer in Progress.
> Please be thoughtful and bring her a biscuit.

The writer is me. DUH. Biscuits used to come at first when Dad thought it was funny. In fact, he would rarely make it up the stairs without a cookie or Jaffa cake in hand but now, not so much. In fact, never. These days biscuits are seen as wonderful treats and sadly not as necessity, because we are becoming deprived and poor. I am forced to continue, much to my disappointment, as a biscuitless genius.

Chapter Two

I first worked out we were running out of money when Mum started buying own-brand stuff from the supermarket. Crisps, sweets, biscuits. But then it got worse . . . more severe. Own-brand tomato sauce. OWN-BRAND TOMATO SAUCE! Then own-brand toothpaste, own-brand washing powder. Enough was enough.

'Are we getting poor?' I ask her at breakfast on Friday.

'DARCY!' Granny snips. 'Don't you DARE ask that!' (This is the granny I don't really like as much as my main most important grandma, so she can jog on, to be honest.)

'Why not? I'm sick of this stupid own-brand cereal. They don't put as much coconut and banana chips in,' I say, ruffling out the banana chips with my fingers.

'We're not getting poor, Darcy' – Mum rubs her eyes with her palms, which she does when she's stressed – 'and DON'T put your hand in the cereal like that. We all eat from that box, thank you very *little*.' (That's Mum's new phrase. It's a play on the phrase *thank you very much*, but you say little because it means you're annoying.)

I eat that handful and then tip the box like a normal person. It's best to be obedient. Dad says I should 'pick my battles' and not just argue over absolutely everything. Sometimes I forget to do this.

'You don't know the meaning of poor, Darcy. Poor is no shelter, no food, no lovely soft posh towels, no TV, no toys, no milk, no tea bags, no bubble bath, no cereal *whatsoever*,' Granny bangs on.

Her voice is like a housefly trapped in my earhole, scratching at my brain. The only real reason the not-as-good granny is here is so that she can pick Poppy and Hector up from school while Mum goes to work for a bit to bring money in. So there, see, I told you. We ARE getting poorer.

That means Granny has been babysitting. For a WHOLE WEEK.

I am NOT a baby.

I know that while she is here she has decided to try and implant these old-fashioned ideas about money in our brains, and to give Mum a good talking to about budgeting and spending like some witch scrooge consultant. I bet Mum had a horrible militant upbringing where she probably wasn't even allowed milk on her porridge, just water. No wonder she and Granny don't get along. It's a total disgrace.

'All right. I get the picture. You didn't need to make me feel so guilty,' I huff.

Granny starts again, *moan moan moan*, while she stirs the ninth sugar into her milky tea. 'When my mother was just a child she lived in a cobble house with only one stove to warm the whole place, and they had one candle that they used as a light and the whole family had to share that candle. They didn't even have a toilet, you had to walk down the road with a bucket,

13

even in the freezing cold or in the middle of the night, just to *spend a penny.** So don't you talk to me about being poor,' Granny mutters.

Who even ASKED her, anyway? There's a very good reason why this granny is not my favourite grandma.

As a reminder, she starts again. 'I used to have dolls made out of wooden spoons in my day. Not like all these dolls upon dolls you and Alice have.'

I roll my eyes. She always gets our names wrong and calls one of us *Alice.* That's our second cousin's name. Our *perfect* second cousin who I can't even be BOTHERED to talk about.

'It's Poppy, Mum,' Mum corrects her.

'That's what I said,' Granny snubs. 'Poppy.'

'No, you called her Alice. Again,' I say, 'and besides, we don't have dolls upon dolls.'

'You do,' Mum argues.

'I don't even like dolls,' I say. 'They don't make dolls with dreadlocks or chopped off dyed-blue hair, and if I liked dolls I would like *those* kinds of dolls.' I obviously sometimes can be partial to a bit of doll

*To spend a penny is Granny language for weeing.

playing, but I don't raise this now.

Granny breathes onto her glasses, to clean them, I guess, but if you ask me it totally defeats the object of cleaning the lenses once her manky old tea breath has covered them in death mist.

BORE OFF.

Whatevs.

OK. So we weren't poor.

But then a yucky guilty sickness starts to trickle up my throat. I feel terrible wretched rotten for saying that now. What a hideous spoiled brat ghoul that is ungrateful I am, moaning about 'own-brand' stuff while other people have nothing. I hate my wicked witch granny for making me feel absolutely wretch- edly horrible about myself.

'Sorry, Mum,' I say. 'There is the exact perfect amount of coconut and chipped banana pieces inside the cereal, and I was just being greedy, and I'm sorry. I am grateful for everything.'

My mum squeezes me in for a big cuddle. 'Money is tight at the moment. Dad's business isn't as busy as normal, he has a lot of backdated payments to chase, and my art isn't really selling . . . so that's why I'm having to do some reception work, remember? To make a bit of extra cash.'

'I understand,' I say. Because I do. Annie, Will's big sister, is always telling me how expensive everything in the world is. We can't all live like my parents' (fake) friends, the Pinchers, throwing money at this and that. I'm sure Mum doesn't want to have to go and sit at a desk in an uncomfortable chair and answer the phone to probably people that are not her species.

Granny pipes up, 'You're too soft on them, Mollie. My mother would have whipped my bottom with a broomstick for talking like that! I would have beaten *your* bottom with a broomstick for talking to *me* like that!'

Mum rolls her eyes, a huge 360-degree eyeball roll. 'You NEVER hit me with a broomstick, Mum.' It's weird hearing my mum saying *Mum* to another lady, especially an old crinkly witch one. 'You never hit me. Not on the bum, not anywhere.'

'Well, that's because I raised you perfectly.' Granny nods. 'There was discipline. There was no need.'

'She is mad.' Mum turns to me right in front of Granny. 'Mad. Mad. Mad as a March hare.'

Mum is quite mad too. Maybe that's because she was raised by Granny. You could go as far as to say that I'm a bit mad too, but I don't really like to acknowledge that there is any trace of Granny in me. Even though technically there can't actually even be a trace of Granny in me or Mum.

Because Mum was adopted. People always think that this means my mum was an unwanted goblin baby in a blanket left under a bridge or something, but it doesn't mean that at all. My mum's real-life mum just couldn't take care of her. That's all. Luckily, Granny took her in and could take care of her, so really Granny can't be *all* that bad. And any time I get mad at her I just must try to remember that she looked after my mum when my mum had no one. But sometimes it's hard when she's being old-fashioned and whiney and whingey and scary to look at . . .

'I can hear you, you know,' Granny clucks.

'Good.' Mum smiles. Granny sips her tea.

What is a Marching Hare anyway?

I get ready to leave for school. Having Granny staying is horror of the head syndrome. I don't even KNOW why Mum HAS to make the effort with her. We don't need a babysitter anyway when we can take perfect exact care of ourselves. I can boil eggs, you know. You just plonk them into the kettle and let them boil in there. It works wonders. I can't stand to be in the house one second longer with moany Granny.

'OK, I'm off.' I go to kiss Mum goodbye.

'But you didn't even finish your cereal,' Granny barks. 'You know what they say, waste not want not!'

'I finished mines.' My littlest and onlyest brother Hector demonstrates this by licking his plate of jam on toast completely clean. What an *animal*. It's so *disturbing*.

But then I hear, 'Oh, me too. I just *can't* possibly even think of concentrating without breakfast. It's the most important precious meal of all time,' Poppy adds, folding her neat tidy hair behind her earlobes, just remaining ridiculously ideal at all times of all day.

I gather my stuff. I have had enough of this doom house made of bricks and cement. I am *not* feeling it, to be honest.

'I will eat something at school,' I say, and now I feel guiltier but I have to get out – it's like the radiators are full blast hot. 'Bye, Granny.' I go in for a kiss because I know if I don't Mum will screwface me.

Granny smells of dried rose petals and lavender and age. Like a ripe plum. 'What's that on your finger, missy?' She points to my hand.

'What? Where?' I am confused.

'That, there.' She puts her glasses over her eyes, peering. Mum looks too.

'What?' I still don't know what she's on about.

'That little warty thing? A bunion? A growth?' She scrunches her face up.

19

I know what she means now. It's a small pea-sized bump on my finger, right under the skin – it doesn't look sore or anything. 'It's always been there . . . well . . . for the last couple of years.'

'That's Darcy's writer's bump,' says Mum.

'A what bump?' Granny parrots.

'Because she's always writing, the pen has made its own little stool to sit on,' Mum beams. 'I'm proud of it.'

I smile. Granny wrinkles up her nose at it. But that just makes me like it even morer.

These days this week with Granny taking care of us are absolute migraine city. She is a wretched beast from the land of Victorian days, like I told you, with old-fashioned rules and policies. Take these examples for yourself if you aren't believing me . . .

Incident one

Picture the scene. It is Monday night, and here I am, just minding my own beeswax watching *Hercules*, one of the greatest Walt Disney films of all time. Lamb-Beth is gently excellently snoring on my tummy.

Granny comes in. 'Your eyes are going square,' she hisses.

'No, they aren't.'

'They are. You've been watching too much television. It's bad for you, that angry box of torture, full of strange and crazy ideas. It melts your brain, you know.'

I try to ignore her. The good bit is coming, where all the excellent ladies with the big bums and boobies begin coming to life around the pot and singing, but CAN I hear it? Of course I can't. Why?

Because Granny won't stop talking. 'Has it made you deaf as well as a square-eyes? Are you listening? The volume is SO high. Kids these days. If my children had even *dreamed* of watching  the television I would have smacked their bottoms with an old boot.'

21

I can't stand it. I get up, switch the TV off and storm out.

She always ruins everything.

One second later and what do I hear? The music of this annoying antiques TV show and her blissfully humming along. I barge back right into the living room.

'What are you doing?' I blurt, my hands on my hips.

'Well, you weren't watching it and my programme is on.'

SEE?

Hypocrite. Mean. Wretched. Old. Bag.

Incident Two

I can't really talk about it, but let's just say I got up in the middle moment of the night for a wee and came face to face in the hall with a ghoul in a pink silk dressing gown. It was wrinkly. It looked like a giant shaved bird. With hollowed-out eyes and no teeth. And hair like dragged-out cotton wool. All in all, like a zombie, shuffling down a hallway. Or like a tired old wee-wee-stained sleeping bag with toes sticking out that looked like dead persons' thumbs painted pearl. Yes. Horrorful.

It was Granny.

I screamed.

Granny screamed back.

It took me hours to get back to sleep.

Incident Three

In general, making us go to bed so early when it's still even light outside.

See how terrible my life is?

On one of these nights I am up in bed. I am FAR from tired. It's still light outside and I just want Mum and Dad to come home to let us get up out of bed and watch TV like how we are supposed to. My belly is twirling from the disgusting gross dinner Granny made us of bacon and liver stew and mashed potatoes with so many lumps in.

I wish my other grandma was here and not this one.

I peel open my writing book.

I write 'Granny' on one side and 'Grandma' on the other. It's the battle of the grans. Which gran will win? Well, I think we BOTH know THAT'S obvious.

GRANNY	GRANDMA
MOANY	NOT THAT MOANY
MEAN	KIND
A HYPOCRITE	NICE
OLD-FASHIONED	TRIES HER BEST
A LIAR	HONEST
NOT GOOD AT CUDDLES	WARM
MAKES GROSS FOOD	MAKES ROAST POTATOES
GIVES US NOTHING	GIVES US MONEY
HATES US	LOVES US

I really REALLY do not even like this granny. I get cross and crosserer and more cross and I just have to really LET IT ALL OUT because I am about to explode out of my skin with madness. I am trying so hard to remember that she looked after my mum, but it's not quite cutting it right now because I'm so brewing livid.

On my bedside table, in my messy room, is a mouldy orange. Yuck. That really has been there a while and oranges take for ever to rot. It's a zombie fruit. Gosh, I am SO angry. I start to scribble. Morer and morer and morer, and then I write:

Gilbert and the Sad-wich

Gilbert was a zombie.

YUCK! Hell, sewage and pain in my eyeballs for the image of Granny in the hall flashes into my head. Maybe I should make the zombie Granny? A woman zombie . . . a vile woman granny zom—

No!

I restrain myself. I'm trying to be positive about Granny. No matter how mean she is.

Instead, Granny can be the victim.

I'm not sure if that's better or not, but I feel more

sorry for her that way. Besides. It's too late now. My Imagination Queen inside my head has made her almighty mind up.

Back to Gilbert.

He was the colour of tangled forest moss, smothered in bluing decaying bruises like squashed-up dank rotted fruit. He groaned. He moaned. He dragged. He slumped.

He was alone.

Being a zombie was sad and hard. There was lots he couldn't do. Like get on a bus or go to the opera or go skiing. Sure, he could perhaps get on a bus but he always seemed to be at the bus stop at the wrong time and he couldn't run. Besides, he didn't trust himself, he would just *have* to eat someone. And he didn't want to do that.

So mostly Gilbert spent his days in the local park. On a bench. All alone. That way he could watch humans from a safe distance. He would raid the local dustbins and try and do anything that would occupy his time. He didn't *WANT* to eat people so he denied the cravings.

One day whilst sitting on the bench, eating the banana skins and dog poo he had found in the bins, an old granny sat down next to him. Gilbert felt nervous. He had never, even in his younger brighter days, been good around old people. He discreetly, without seeming rude, tried to walk away. He was always a polite boy, even as a zombie.

'Don't mind me,' the granny said. 'You sit yourself down, young boy.'

Gilbert stopped, lurched in his tracks.

'Come on, sit yourself down, I don't bite,' the granny giggled. She smelled disgusting. Of flowers and petals and herbs and cake.

Gilbert groaned.

'You moody teenager, what are you like?' the granny tutted. 'Youth today, always moaning when there is nothing to be moaning about. You've got your whole entire life ahead of you.'

Gilbert groaned. This human was VERY
annoying.

'If it's not one thing,' the granny continued,
'it's another. You don't know how lucky you are.
In MY day we didn't have anything. These
days, children are spoiled for choice.'

Gilbert groaned.

'Will you not sit down? Look at you! You
need more sleep, you've been a night owl,
haven't you? And your skin is so ghastly,
that will be those fizzy drinks and tutti-fruttis,
no doubt, and look at your nails! Do you
bite those? You should leave them to soak in
vinegar, then you won't bite them, I tell you!
And you're so thin, you should eat, here, do
you like ham sandwiches?'

Gilbert didn't like ham sandwiches. He didn't
really like to eat anything other than human
beings, but free ham was better than raiding the
bins, as that was exhausting and his energy was
running low.

Gilbert used all of his strength to plonk

himself down next to the granny with a deflated defeated puff. His hunger was like a wild animal now. He was thirsty too. For blood and guts. And suddenly he could smell the granny. That she was human. That her heart was beating.

'Take this, go on . . .' The granny offered him the sandwich. It was little, squished a bit from lying at the bottom of her handbag. It was wrapped in cellophane. White bread. Pink thin ham.

It looked sad.

A sad-wich.

And Gilbert, without thinking, couldn't help himself, watching her little thin speckled frail wrist hold out the sandwich to him. He just opened his mouth and ate the granny.

She screamed, but at least she shut up. She was so annoying.

A man walking his dog saw. And then ran. Probably for the best.

OK. So it didn't go exactly as planned. Granny gets eaten.

But at least I have dispelled my anger to some degree. And there it remains. Privately. In my writing book. Where my feelings cannot hurt anybody.

Chapter Three

Thank the dinosaurs that at last now it is Friday. Which means I am in an excellent mood. Mum's done her week of temping as a receptionist, which means my ugly needle of a hypocrite granny will be shoving off back to her boring old wee-wee house tomorrow morning.

Will and I walk to class together. He won't stop going on about how '*This time next week we'll be at the school sleepover blah blah blah.*' It's so annoying. I still haven't told him that I really don't want to go. I wish we could just do our own thing, but then he reveals a chocolate mousse from the inside of his blazer and my mood suddenly evaporates.

'Want a dip?' he asks.

'Sure.' I dip my finger in the mousse and wind it round, collecting it all up like a human spoon.

'Oi!' Will shrieks. 'I said a dip, not a forklift truckful!'

'Calm down!' I laugh, and then he wipes his finger on my cheek. Gross. We begin to fight, wrestling with the chocolate mousse and it's flying everywhere.

Clementine, YUCK, trots over with her stupid wretched mashed potato-headed boyfriend Olly Supperidge. These two are my worserest people on the planet, except Olly runs the school magazine and so SOMETIMES we have to speak because I write for it. Even though I MUCHER preferred doing business with Koala who seems to have been kicked out. Clementine turns her trot into a canter and, swishing her pony hair about, says, 'Darcy, just a word of advice, I couldn't help noticing that you guys just both *double-dipped* in the single pot of chocolate mousse. It's really unhygienic.' She pulls a really grossed-out face. Olly catches up with her, galloping behind like a drunken donkey.

'More or less hygienic than you two snogging all day long?' Will snorts, and I laugh.

'Actually less. Much less,' Olly blurts. 'The mouth is one of the most hygienic parts of the human body. Whereas fingers . . . well . . . they are totally riddled with bacteria.'

The bell rings for first class. Clementine, unfortunately, is in our class, but Olly is not because he is older – although you wouldn't know it as his behaviour is worserer than Hector's. Clementine and Olly then begin to say goodbye to each other as though it's their last day on earth together. I don't know where to look, it's hideous.

'Not as riddled as your breath,' Will giggles. 'Brush your teeth before school, seriously, mate, or you'll give Clementine a disease!' And then we begin to laugh. Even though two wrongs don't make a right, I know, but they deserve it. And it's JOKES.

'This isn't over, William Hopper! Mark my words!' Olly shouts, all show-offy because he can walk backwards and hold a conversation at the same time.

The three of us reluctantly head into English

together. There is a terrific audible buzz in the entire classroom and I know it's all because of this silly whole entire school sleepover. And it's just about to get worse.

'I'm sure some of you have noticed,' Mr Yates begins, 'that the charity sleepover is just a week away.'

To that everybody stomps their feet as if going to the sleepover automatically rewards us with two birthdays a year instead of one for the rest of our lives. Honestly. I roll my eyes.

'I'm sure you've all been very busy choosing your pyjamas . . . I for one have a lovely onesie lined up!' Everybody laughs at this – Mr Yates can sometimes be a joker. 'But I wanted to bring your attention to the talent competition. We've seen a huge number of entries, hands up if you've entered . . .' A few hands sprout up. Clementine's is first to shoot up, no doubt. No surprise there. 'That's great.' Mr Yates smiles. 'But nobody, *not one student*, is entering any of their written work. We have nothing to represent the astounding standard of literacy we produce here at school, and that's such a shame. Remember, it's not a competition, it's a celebration of talent. I mean, we have talented singers, dancers, magicians coming out of our ears – but writers . . . I mean . . . come on, where are you hiding?'

Will nudges me.

I ignore his nudges.

He nudges me again and whispers, 'You should read something.'

'Shut up,' I growl back. I don't even want to go, let alone READ. In FRONT of the ENTIRE school? Are you mad?

'Go on, you could write something and read it, it would be epic, you'd be the best!' he hisses.

'Will, it's *not* a competition, and no . . . I—'

Mr Yates stops the class. 'Care to share with the rest of us your private conversation with Miss Burdock, William?'

Will shakes his head.

'So, don't interrupt my lesson then.'

'Sorry, sir.' Will blushes, and I shrink. 'It's just . . .'

No. Will. DO NOT. DO NOT DO IT.

'I was just saying to Darcy, I really think she should enter the talent show. She should read some of her writing. I mean, I think . . . like not in a weird way or anything . . . but she's a really good writer, and so sorry for interrupting but that's what I was saying.'

NO. NO. NO. NO. I am so embarrassed. Everybody stares me up and down. NO.

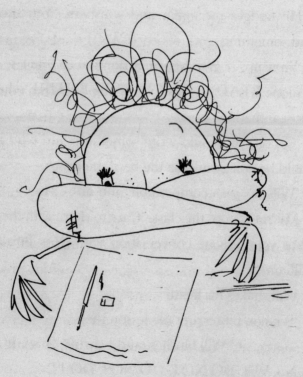

Mr Yates smiles. 'I think that's not a bad idea at all, Will. I think Darcy is an exceptionally talented writer and would do our literary department proud.'

I am so nervous and shy that I'm not even taking the words in and everybody is looking at me for a response and then suddenly Clementine pipes up.

'Well, actually, the lyrics of my song are quite poetic and moving. I actually think I would do justice for music and English, and I mean, I think I'm more of full final polished talent than Darcy. I mean, no offence, but I've kind of got it all, and when it comes to live performance, sadly, looks count too. In this ugly world a spot of beauty goes a very long way, don't you think?'

I cannot believe my ears. She has been spending far too much time with Olly Supperidge.

Mr Yates laughs Clementine's comment off, even though she is right. Clementine is conditioned and shiny and glossy and fake and plastic like a new car, and I am clumsy and shy and have knotty hair and bumps on my arms and bruises on my knees like a battered old camper van.

'Darcy, what do you say? Would you read some of your own writing?' he says to me.

The words jump out before I can jump into the dark box in my head. 'No. I don't think so.'

'You can lead a horse to water, Mr Yates, but you can't make it drink,' Clementine snarls. 'I promise to deliver, Mr Yates.'

I hate her.

And you're not even meant to do hating.

Will looks at me, disappointed.

The rest of the lesson is a blur. I am not listening, just panicking about this stupid sleepover. What will I even wear? I have a wardrobe full of the most mental pyjamas in the history of pyjamas. I never ever *ever* expected anyone outside of my family would see them. Mum is still certain she is not NEVER EVER NEVER going to let me get new pyjamas. Not when we 'barely have two pennies to rub together'. As Dad is forever telling me.

I chew nearly all my nails off from anxiety. I can't go. I'm not going to go. I've made my mind up. I will stay indoors and eat a pillowcase stuffed full of Maltesers and pretend that I am a magical mermalade enjoying my glorious life, and just as class is winding to an end Mr Yates finishes with, 'And if you're performing or not, remember the sleepover is for charity, so I expect to see everybody's faces, no excuses.'

And to that Clementine adds, 'Exactly! You've all had an invite, so you're basically a selfish scum of the earth if you don't come! We've put a LOT of effort into organizing this event!'

Mr Yates chuckles awkwardly again at Clementine and her bonkers personality. She is TOO much. BLEUGH.

But I have to go, don't I? If not, I am scum of the earth. Packing my stuff up, I try and scramble to catch up with Will. Perhaps if I choose my words cleverly I can be an evil dark fairy of persuasion and convince him to make a secret den with me on the night of the sleepover so we don't have to endure the horrors of Clementine.

Then I feel her before I see her. Clementine. Her voice crackles up the back of my neck. That demon fruit. She's trying to be nice. It's ghastly. It's like watching a slug trying to jump.

'I can't WAIT to see your pyjamas, Darcy.'

I gulp.

'I'm sure you have some proper *crazy random* ones. CUTE!'

'Yeah.' I nod.

'And make sure you stick around. I mean, I know you don't have the confidence to share your talent, which is a shame, but at least let me share mine with you! Can't WAIT for you to hear my voice.'

OH WHY?

OH WHY?

OH WHY?

THIS LIFE.

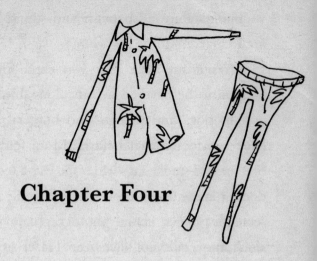

Chapter Four

'NO!' says Mum. 'NO. NO. NO. NO. NO. NO.'

'But please,' I cry. Not real tears, but certainly excellent crocodile ones. I mean, I was GOING for it.

'I said you can go, isn't that enough?' Mum nearly shouts.

I don't even want to go. How has this ended up backfiring? But I feel if I say now that I don't want to go Mum will think it's all about the pyjamas and then she will feel guilty.

'I'm not buying you new pyjamas or a stupid onesie for one night when you've got so many good sets already.' She shakes her head.

'But they are all babyish and stupid and ugly,' I argue.

'It's not my fault that you chose pyjamas that happen to be covered in ridiculous things like cacti and hotdogs and planets and burgers! You should have considered that before.' Mum folds her arms. She used to smoke fags when she was a teenager – she doesn't know that I know but, *oh I know, all right*. I've seen *photographs*: actual photographic evidence. See, so Granny could not have been THAT strict. At times like this, when she's annoyed, I think she would love nothing more than to pull out a big fat cigarette and smoke it down in one go.

Granny pipes up again, 'I don't understand how you can even let her go, Mollie. A night in a hall, boys and girls *mixed*. Anything could happen! I don't like the sound of it.'

'Thanks a lot, Granny,' I say with sarcasm.

She ignores me and begins to give me some unwanted *advice*. 'The last thing you want is to play a game of Spin the Twig and end up having to sit in a corner while a boy whispers sweet nothings into your ear. One thing will lead to another, and next thing you know he will be wanting to take you to the school dance and then he will be wanting to share half a lager and lemonade with you in the local tavern, singing Frankie Valli and the Four Seasons' *My Eyes Adored You* into your eyes, and before you know it, that will be you, stuck in the kitchen peeling potatoes and making gravy and babies for the rest of your life.' Granny sips her tea. 'Can happen to anybody.'

Mum and I don't say anything, except exchange a slow blink.

'Any-way. *Moving* on. Darcy . . .'

Mum chuckles awkwardly in a laugh that I didn't even know she had in her catalogue of laughter. 'I've said you can go to the sleepover, but just this morning I was telling you that money was tight. I haven't got money for a new pair of pyjamas for you when you've got so many. It's unreasonable.'

'I just . . .' I don't want to cry, because this is a silly baby reason to cry. But Clementine's noodle-hair-framed face is just bobbing about in my imagination, laughing at all my *crazy 'random'* nightwear and saying, *You'll be the scum of the earth, the scum of the earth, the scum of the earth* . . . 'I. Just. Don't want to look like a freak.'

'Good luck with that.' Poppy trots in. She is drinking juice from a carton and has chewed the straw so much it doesn't even resemble a straw any more. My sadness immediately turns into rage.

'Shut up,' I say. 'You're just jealous.'

'Yeah, right,' Poppy spits back.

'Why doesn't Darcy want to wear any of her pyjamas?' Mum tries to reason with Poppy. 'I don't understand.'

'She wants to wear something *sexy*,' Poppy laughs.

'NO I DON'T!' I flush red with embarrassment.
I DO NOT!

'Borrow something of mine,' says
Granny. 'You should wear fleece.
Best to be safe. A nice rollneck and
socks and mittens to match.'

'FLEECE!' I splutter. Even
Lamb-Beth looks just about
ready to vom.

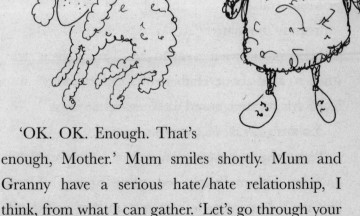

'OK. OK. Enough. That's
enough, Mother.' Mum smiles shortly. Mum and
Granny have a serious hate/hate relationship, I
think, from what I can gather. 'Let's go through your
drawers, Darcy, and see what you've got.'

'I know I don't have anything,' I grumble.

'I don't know why you care, Darcy. You're always so confident with your clothes.' Mum looks, for the first time, concerned about my clothes. I don't like the look she is giving me. It's all serious all of a sudden. I'm not surprised she's confused. I don't even know myself what I even want.

'I think it's healthy to address the way you dress, Darcy. Sometimes you do look rather . . . garish,' Granny says, while checking out her own outfit of wool and beige in the mirror.

GARISH? GARISH! HOW DARE SHE!

Mum rolls her eyes suitably and says to me, 'Is something the matter?'

I don't know what to say to that. I know she is right. I never cared about 'clothes rules' before today.

I have always ignored those stupid sayings:

Red and green should never be seen.

I have the best green jumper that looks completely amazing with my bright red velvet leggings. It looks like the exact image of Christmas, but apparently that's what is so bad about it. Who DOESN'T want to look like a Christmas elf? Huh?

Spots or stripes, but not together.

What a complete joke! Why wouldn't you wear two of the most best patterns together? Doesn't make any sense to me at all.

And *Less is more.*

That's the most worst bit of advice I've ever heard. You've only got one life. This is just something I feel totally passionate about, and while Mum goes to brown the shepherd's pie in the oven I do a bit of writing . . .

The Eventful Exploration of Ray Beam
All about a man who dressed like the sun.

Mr Ray Beam was a businessman. I don't know what he did — it doesn't even matter — but he worked in the central heart of the city where the cars beeped louder and you have to walk like cement; slow, and filling in all the gaps.

   Mr Ray Beam had just got his first ever job in the city. *Wowza.* Sooo flashy. It was very exciting. And he got moved to an even taller, most exciting and established building, or so he thought, but really it was terrible. So grey and so boring. The building was very tall, nearly

reaching the clouds, and was covered in huge windows, but you could not see out of them and you couldn't see in either.

'That's pointless,' Mr Ray Beam muttered to himself when he found out, and he instantly instructed his secretary to put some nature there: some plants and flowers would do nicely.

On his first day he decided to dress to impress. Mr Ray Beam believed that it was very important to dress to match your personality, so that your character shined, even through your clothes. Mr Ray Beam was a very positive and uplifting member of society and decided that to show his new members of staff and colleagues what he was truly like he would have to go for bright orange trousers, a bright yellow shirt, a red tie and an electric-blue jacket. He even thought that red stripy socks would set the outfit off a treat.

It is important to mention that Mr Ray Beam lived alone, so there was nobody to be like, 'Hey, what do you think about this outfit?' to, and his sausage dog,

Burger, was too busy tearing up a deck of cards to care.

At 6.30 a.m., because business people's lives start horrifically horribly early, Mr Ray Beam set off for his first day of work. He never minded the early starts. 'Rise and shine, just like the sun,' he nodded to himself, swinging his briefcase and whistling down the road to the station.

Next Mr Ray Beam found himself completely cramped on a squished train carriage. Everybody was dressed head to toe in grey and navy and black. He felt like a rogue yellow crayon amongst a pack of grey HB pencils. His face was smushed into a big fat teddy bear of a man with breath like a dustbin truck and armpit juice like sewage, but Mr Ray Beam did not mind, not even when a mean stern-looking office lady in a 'I'D DIE FOR MY JOB' power suit splashed latte down his orange trousers.

Walking down the busy street, he tried his best to swing his briefcase as he so liked to do, but it just wasn't easy because people were everywhere, swarming like iron filings to a magnet.

'Never mind,' Mr Ray Beam said to himself as the people nudged him, all charging and marching in the same exact direction, not stopping even once to make eye contact with one another; they were like worker bees, just accessorized with umbrellas and mobile phones and newspapers.

Mr Ray Beam *always* used a spinny door

at posh offices or shopping centres. He was NOT mental, he would NEVER take a regular standard door and he took great pride in twisting round the spinny door and, occasionally, wouldn't think twice of going round a second time just for the novelty. Which never wore off.

Beaming broadly to the receptionist about the *fine* day, he headed upstairs in the lift where he was close to bursting with excitement.

'Did you feel the butterflies in your tummy on *your* first day?' he asked the people in the lift with him, but they all ignored him and stared at their phones.

In his first meeting, around a large table where the biscuits were too far to reach, Mr Ray Beam awkwardly tried not to look at the bogey hanging out of the talking man's nostril, the toothpaste lurking in the corners of another's mouth, the bulging tum of a big grumpy man with a hairpiece flapped over his balding head, and couldn't help but think to himself . . .

Why can't you lot dress like *yourselves*?

Over bitter coffee and with, as imaginable, extreme coffee breaths, the meeting ended with a puff of sincere disappointment, and then, as quickly as kids in a classroom once the bell goes for lunch, they all rushed out.

Mr Ray Beam drained the last drop from his carton of freshly squeezed orange juice and followed them out. He was like a parrot among an army of pigeons.

The days grinded past, weeks dragged like a suitcase full of chopped-up planet Jupiter with no wheels. Yes, Mr Ray Beam did his work just fine, but nobody wanted to have lunch with him at the cool burrito joint — they all wanted packaged cardboard sandwiches in the awkward staff room. Nobody wanted to throw a Frisbee round the park — they all just wanted to nip to the gym to run like a hamster on a wheel for twenty minutes. This was bringing Mr Ray Beam down a bit.

'I think this is bringing me down a bit,' he announced that evening to his dog, Burger, who farted and rolled over. 'Yes, me too.' Mr Ray Beam acknowledged Burger. 'Do you think I should continue to dress like the sunshine?'

And Burger got up, stretched, picked up his bone and buried it deep into the arm of the sofa.

'I appreciate the feedback, Burger. I think so too.'

The next morning Mr Ray Beam was called into the HEAD OFFICE.

'Morning, guys!' Mr Ray Beam clapped his hands breezily. He had a glass bottle of milk, which he drank directly from the bottle, so it

left him with an
IMMATURE milk
moustache, which
he knew was there
but did not
remove.

Ha
Ha
Hee

'Don't tell me, I've got
a milktache!' he chuckled,
but the others in HEAD OFFICE did NOT.

'Mr Beam,' one of them began. His gums were
black.

'Call me Ray, please.'

'Mr Beam,' the Black Gums Man said again.
'Your work clothes are annoying people.'

'I beg your pardon?' Mr Ray Beam tried to
laugh this comment off. 'Sir, these are not my
work clothes.'

'Fine, your *fancy-dress costume.*'

'This is not a costume either, sir. These are
my actual real clothes.'

'I don't care if they were stitched together by Cinderella herself – they are distressing and distracting and disgusting, and we all hate them and we want you to dress *normal*,' the Black Gums Man spat.

'Normal?' Mr Ray Beam looked confused. 'What is *normal*?'

A man with noodle needle thin round glasses sensed tension. He took over as the man with the black gums was getting hot and flustered.

'I think what Sir is trying to say is . . . perhaps try dressing like . . . yourself?' Glasses Man *tried* to reason.

'That *is* what I'm doing.' Mr Ray Beam

proudly demonstrated his outfit by putting his
hands on his hips and twirling as if he was on
a catwalk. The *others* seemed unimpressed.

'Well, clearly not.' Glasses Man laughed
sarcastically in frustration. 'I don't think your
clothing is . . . *professional* . . .'

'Mr Beam . . .' A woman
took on from here. She had
a dark grey bob and was
wearing a pearly shade of
hideous eye shadow that
made her look like a ghoul
from a horror film. 'This is
a working environment,' she
soothed, 'so we need the correct attire that
shows your skill. Why not try something smart
and clean and simple? Dark shades to flatter?'
She attempted a weak and feeble smile.

'Something to not . . . how shall I put this?
Stand out . . .' a big woman added. She was
as tall as nearly the ceiling, with tincy nostrils.
(Mr Ray Beam wished Burger were here to

witness how small her nostrils actually were.
She was so tall too — surely she needed a lot
more breath than what those holes could permit.
Nature could be *so* cruel.)

'Something that *blends* in, that doesn't . . .
shall we say . . . *make a statement*. Draw
attention. Give the wrong impression. Send the
wrong message?' Glasses Man said again.
He was so smarmy and condescending and
snakelike. Mr Ray Beam didn't hate anybody,
but this guy was on the verge of being a bit
hated.

'So you're asking me to dress like YOUR self?
Not MY self at all?' Mr Ray Beam confronted
them.

'No, not at all. We want you to dress like
yourself. Just think, less *clown*?' the Woman
With the Bob suggested. The carefully chosen
words were annoying Mr Ray Beam. If they
were going to crush him, at least they should
stomp properly rather than tiptoeing around
the edges.

'More robot?' Mr Ray Beam said.

'Less *sunny*?' the Tall Tiny-Nostrilled Lady suggested.

'More windy, rainy with a chance of thunder?' Mr Ray Beam quizzed sarcastically.

'I'm sick of beating around the bush on this one!' the Big Boss spluttered. 'Just stop dressing so happy! You look ridiculous!'

'So, you want me to dress *sad*, then.' Mr Ray Beam understood. He understood perfectly. They didn't want him to dress bright and colourful because they didn't want him to be happy. *Wow*

'Stop being so pathetic and emotional, man, you're too sensitive,' the Big Boss boomed. 'Now, you were promoted for a reason, and there's a big project coming up and I need you to deliver, so no more clowning about! Understood?'

Mr Ray Beam felt flattened like a hedgehog on the motorway. 'Understood,' he sighed gently.

Mr Ray Beam trudged home to Burger, who was waiting for him on the sofa. Together, they packed his wonderful bright colourful clothes into a suitcase. I say together, but Burger mostly just blinked and sniffed.

'Well, that's that then, Burger. Now tell me what you think of these new suits I got today.'

They were black and navy and grey and brown and straight and normal and identical to every pigeon in his office. Burger growled at the sight of them.

'Me too.' Mr Ray Beam nodded. 'Horrible. Just horrible.'

The days dragged harder than ever before, the weeks inched ahead, like trying to pull a tractor across a field of gluey mud with just your little finger. Mr Ray Beam's happiness was being blotted out more and more. But it was undeniable that he was a very, very good worker and particularly good at his job, even if it did mean that he couldn't get to wear his usual kaleidoscope attire.

At the office, the clock ticked.

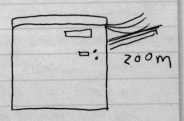

The photocopier zoomed. The phone rang. The clouds creamed over the sky.

Mr Ray Beam was fading away.

People became greyer, paler, darker.

The office walls became dirtied, as if tea stains were leaving inky brown rings on them. The phone rang less. It was a miserable place to be.

Then one day he noticed the Woman with the Bob had made her hair slightly lighter, just a shade or so. It made her look happier. But he didn't compliment her. He wanted to, but he resisted temptation. *She doesn't deserve it*, he thought to himself.

Then he noticed that the Glasses Man had got a new pair of specs, stripy coloured ones. He even overheard the Woman with the Bob compliment him by the coffee machine. The Glasses Man said he knew they were a bit 'out there' and 'crazy' but 'why not, eh? You only live once!' He defended his fashion splurge, and they cackled together.

Then Mr Ray Beam noticed that the Tall Tiny-Nostrilled Lady was wearing a big bow in her hair. He heard her say that *the office had*

suddenly become duller than ever,
as if a cloud had eternally shoved
itself right in front
of the sun and it
made her
feel low. 'I
just had to
do something about
it,' she chuckled, 'so
I got myself this giant
big purple hair bow, I
mean, I know it's a
bit wacky but I was out of solutions!'

Then some of the other colleagues began to
dress up themselves, in shiny earrings, shiny
watches, shiny nail varnish, shiny stockings, a
little bit of shiny here and there. Mr Ray Beam
spotted it more and more. Like a magpie, he
clocked these tiny details; at first just the
titchy things — colourful shoelaces, a dotty
spotty tie, a neckerchief covered in flowers, but
then a little more . . .

People were missing his colour right before his very eyes, and they began to gather around his desk. 'Could I get your advice on this please, Mr Beam?' they would say, holding up a very important file. 'What is your opinion on this, Ray?' another might say, waving a juicy big document his way. 'Yes or no to this?' another asked him (but that was just somebody asking for his feedback on a pair of glittery platform boots).

People began to say 'Hello' to each other and 'How are you?' and then 'You look nice'. And 'Thanks, mate' and then asking to spend lunch times together in the park playing Frisbee and eating burritos instead of sandwiches.

'What's going on?' the Big Boss hissed. 'This place has become a joke shop!' He hammered his fists on the boring brown desk.

'I'm afraid the figures speak for themselves, sir,' Colourful Glasses Man said in a much chirpier voice.

'Mr Ray Beam was an excellent investment,

and his input to the team has been astounding,' added the Woman with the Multi-coloured Bob.

'He has made a complete colourful impression on everybody, in fact. A dose of sunshine was exactly what we needed in this dull grey office, and because we are happier, we are working harder,' the Tall Tiny-Nostrilled Lady said, then took off her stilts and was actually just four foot six inches. 'It's been hard wearing these, my legs were aching. I've been trotting around in these for years as I was worried you wouldn't take me seriously and might fire me if you knew.' She breathed in deep relief, and everybody looked at her, astonished. 'But yes, my nostrils are really just this tiny though.'

A power from a higher place booted the Big Boss out of his job. He was given the option of wearing a mermaid costume every day or quitting, and he chose the latter. The shoes needed to be filled by somebody else and who better than a big ray of light, Mr Ray Beam.

He didn't fill those shoes, though; he got new ones, bright green ones with pink laces.

And his first new rule was to make those windows *pointmore*, which is obviously the opposite of pointless.

I smile when I think of Mr Ray Beam, but for some reason the idea of wearing my octopus pyjamas or doughnut nightie or mermaid onesie or unicorn costume with horn and tail is making me feel embarrassed and sick to the stomach with nerves. And I don't know why. I feel all icky and itchy and hot. Or maybe that's the image of Granny in her 'fleece'. Yeah, it's probably that, to be fair.

But then I feel sad. Because even though I just writted this story, and even though no matter how much I adore Mr Ray Beam, I know that I am a cowardly girl that wants to just, for once, be a bit normal. I don't want to stand out like a sored thumb. I don't want Clementine to laugh at me. A bit I just want to fit in like everybody else and I can't help hate myself a little bit for it. I am shrinking.

Dad walks in from work. He is digging at his mound of reheated shepherd's pie in a piping hot bowl. He spies Mum, Poppy, Hector and me under a mountain of pyjamas. Hector is swamped underneath the pile, throwing things everywhere. Granny is watching us, and I know she is secretly fighting off all old lady tendencies to scoop all these clothes up and either whisk them off to the charity shop or turn them into some sort of old lady patchwork quilt.

'Are we doing a jumble sale?' Dad laughs.

'Darcy's got a pyjama party.'

'Well, you've got enough here to dress *everybody*.'

'My point exactly.' Mum itches her head, she is stressed.

'I don't, Dad. All these are babyish, and I need proper ones. It's a party; it's like exactly the same as a party where I would wear a nice dress except it's in pyjamas. I can't wear just *any* pyjamas; they have to be good ones. Like, REALLY good ones.'

'What are you talking about?' Dad jokes. 'You've got incredible pyjamas. Look at them.' He dumps his bowl of slop on the side, shakes off his rain-sodden work jacket and picks up my *CRASH, BANG, WALLOP* pyjamas, a basic twin set with *CRASH, BANG, WALLOP* scribbled all over them. 'How cool are these?' he

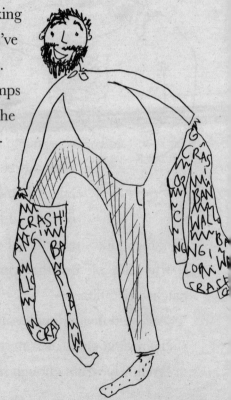

68

laughs, and begins to put them on. His arms are too long for them because the sleeves are so short. We hear a big splitting noise as he tries to wrangle his elbows into the arms and we all begin to laugh. 'Told you! Or what about this?' He picks up my kangaroo onesie – it even has a tail and a baby that sits inside the pouch, all snug. He begins to shove his legs in the trouser holes, squeezing his big oversized feet in and wobbling around. 'Aargh! Watch out!'

'They are too small!' Hector shouts. 'You're too big, Daddy!'

'Yes, well maybe I have grown a tad.' He pokes his slightly bulging belly and wibble wobbles some more and falls into the heap of clothes, nearly dragging the curtains down with him. We all laugh, but not Granny.

'I've brought my sewing machine!' she beams, delighted.

We all have a quiet moment of thought.

The curtains from the spare room are underneath the sharp needle of the sewing machine, battering them to resemble arms and legs. Granny has her glasses on, a few pins in her mouth and is squinting her eyes, her whole body at an angle. I am standing on a chair with Mum pressing a bajillion odd pins into the material around me, a tape measure wrapped around my neck and actual pins and needles in my feet from standing in the same position for so long. Granny has written my measurements on scraps of little yellow paper from her diary all over me in squares. I'm thinking . . . *Isn't she going to NEED those pages in her diary? How will she know what the future will hold?* Or maybe she wants to take each day as it comes. I accept that. Then again . . . what plans does she even have?

Monday: Eat some yoghurt. Be annoying. Have a cup of tea. Moan. Do a crossword. Tell someone off for doing nothing wrong. Have a cup of tea. Give my opinion that nobody wants. Stroke next-door neighbour's cat. Even though it does not want to be stroked. Grimace. Have a cup of tea. Complain. Purchase some skin-coloured tights. Steal sweets off grandchildren. Have a cup of tea. Sigh. Deeply. Annoy my grandchildren with comparisons of the past. Probs just have another cup of tea to be safe.

Poppy is being a brute and is purposely doing annoying hyperactive *doing* actions on the floor which she would never normally do but is thoroughly enjoying as I have to stay still.

CURTAINS. I AM WEARING CURTAINS.

'They won't look like curtains,' Mum reassures me. 'Not once they are finished and ironed. They will be really smart.'

Dad raises his eyebrows doubtfully, like, REALLY?

Lamb-Beth is burrowing into the scraps of odd ends of curtain that have fallen away from the machine, nibbling and rolling and just generally being really completely cute.

'Stay still,' Mum mutters – she sure is bossy when Granny is in town!

'I am!'

'You're not, look at you. Jelly on a plate.'

'I was imagining I was on a surfboard and I was

71

a surfer,' I say, which I was, privately, in my head.

'Well, don't.'

Poppy flutters her eyes. 'I am imagining I am the ballerina inside the jewellery box that spins around and around when you open it up.' She closes her eyes and twirls around.

'Butter wouldn't melt,' Mum laughs with sarcasm at Poppy.

'Butter wouldn't melt? What does that mean?' I ask Mum.

'Butter wouldn't melt in her mouth. It means, look how cute she is trying to be . . . she looks as though she just could NEVER do anything wrong! When we know *otherwise*.'

Yes, we do.

Poppy is oblivious to the butter chat. 'Look how graceful I am, laaa, laaa, daaa, deee, laaa . . .' and then she falls into the table and *Bam* . . . !

The tub of pins spills onto the floor. There must be at least one trillion thousand and fourteen pins now, all over the carpet. It's even more annoying than when I once dropped a whole box of Coco Pops because at

least you can pick them up and eat them a bit, or get
Lamb-Beth and Hector to hoover them up with their
mouths like anteaters, but PINS . . . PINS . . . you
have to be so CAREFUL with them because they can
stab you.

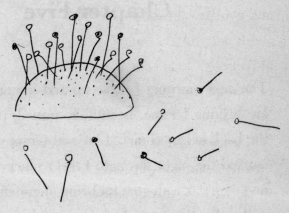

Chapter Five

The next morning I wake up and my new pyjamas are waiting for me, beautifully ironed, perfectly, on the back of my chair. Mum and Granny must have worked the night through. I feel so lucky and loved, and then sick with guilt for being ungrateful yesterday, and realize that actually the time and effort they spent making my pyjamas cancels out all the money pushed together in the world.

I roll them out and they are really cool. They are navy and white striped, and a lovely thick curtain material but not one bit itchy. Already a huge weight has been lifted from my heavy worn down shoulders. I mean, I'd still prefer not to go, but at least now I have something to wear.

But when I try them on and look in the mirror a much far worserer feeling slithers down my throat and into my body. Spoiling all traces of happiness. This isn't who I am! Not at all! I am like Ray Beam, the colourful parrot amongst the pigeons. What am I doing even wearing boring old saddo maddo depressive curtain-jams when I am meant to be a tropical rainbow? But it's too late. They've gone to all this trouble now, haven't they? I feel like I can physically see the blood, sweat and tears in my granny's stitches. Oh, I HATE me for my mid-child-crisis emotional breakdown that made me doubt myself.

I decide to think about this later. Once Granny is out of sight, out of mind, I can make a proper decision.

Granny is going home today. Thank goodness. She lives in an area that is 'quite a drive away', with cows and pigs and goats and grass. In a tincy village where everybody knows each other's names and the baker is actually a baker, like not just an anybody that doesn't look you in the eye and serves you warmed (from frozed up) sausage rolls. She has to get the train.

It's a Saturday, so we don't have to rush or be annoyed about anything.

We take Granny to the station. It's a busy one where lots of so much is happening, people saying *hello* and *goodbye*, hugging and waving. I don't even know where all these people have come from. There they all are, rushing and carrying and dragging lots of luggage and baggage, barging past one another or talking on the phone. Some people have pets, but nobody has a Lamb-Beth, *so there*, and when I get home and lay my eyes on my lamb I will remind her of her special outlandish importance to me.

Granny buys a tea and a slice of fruitcake. She moans about how 'dear' London prices are for the fourteen hundredth time today. Then she decides she would also like a salmon and cucumber sandwich and a packet of crisps, for the train. I can't even believe she eats crisps. Crisps don't suit her one bit. If I imagined her eating a snack it would be like a brandy snap or a Hovis biscuit or something as close to dog biscuits as possible. I imagine all the grains of salt clinging to her wrinkles around her dog-bum mouth, possibly being stuck there for an ever, like pearls inside oyster shells.

Her train is ready, and after complaining about the *distance* of the platform, she takes turns to say goodbye to us, her furry face a wall of powder and as delicate as the wing of a butterfly. Her shoes click-clack on the marble floor of the station and she waves again, Dad trailing behind her with her luggage. Mum is beaming and blowing kisses towards her that she doesn't even mean, I don't think, and as the train pulls away Mum drops her shoulders.

'Phew, glad that's over,' she sighs under her breath. I *SO* knew those kisses were not sincere.

Mum is now in high spirits and wants to enjoy the day with us. It feels weird that Granny went home on a Saturday morning, the only day we *all* had off and were free to play with her, but I'm not complaining. She is one ANNOYING EVIL granny. Dad suggests all the things we could do, but as it's raining, as per usual in London, Mum says she would love nothing more than to get some lovely food and make a big lunch with her family and wrap up and watch a film together. We ALL know that won't be a reality, because we will all want to watch a different film.

We go to the supermarket and we get a big trolley. Hector sits at the front in the little chair bit, and Poppy clambers inside too and I get jealoused because I want to squish in too but Mum says that I'm too big and not allowed. I feel all clumsy and wretched and oversized and huge, and even fat a bit for a second, which I never normally feel, but it's only because I'm not small any more like my brother and sister.

I get over that quickly as the supermarket is the worst place to even consider feeling fat. Mum gets salad things and we pick what apples we like the look of, without bruises, and shiny ones obvs. You have to choose apples that would only appear in fairy tales. You have to think to yourself, 'Would Snow White choose this apple?' And if the answer is yes, then it's yours. We put the apples in the bags and Dad knots them up for us. We have separate apple bags to avoid confusion; so nobody gets snide and gets tempted by the other's apple and also to avoid contamination of one another's gross unbearable lurgies. The apple politics are *quite* an ordeal.

I don't want to bring up the money business at all, and do my best not to pick out any treats or unnecessary nonsense in case one of my parents loses it. Then we have a fight using the apples in cellophane bags as weapons, and all the apples get bruised and one tumbles out onto the floor, and Dad gets cross at us and we have to choose our apples all over again. We just put the bished and bashed ones back in the crates for some idiot who isn't paying attention to scoop up, and that will be their fault for not taking their own personal time and attention to find an 'only fit for Snow White appealing apple'.

Poppy is out of the trolley by now and is going berserk in the yoghurt section. We get fresh crusty bread and cheese and ham and soup and crisps and croissants and shampoo, and cat litter for Pork, and biscuits for Lamb-Beth, and a big bottle of diet Coke. So LOTS of treats basically. I feel like telling Mum and Dad that we don't need all that, that we don't mind just eating cereal for every meal but I know that it would only make Dad sad mixed in with angry because he always puts us first and would never want us to go without the things we like. I get scared when we get to the cashier, even though that's one of my most likely jobs that I would like to be (other than a writer or a customer or a grandad or a spy) because all day long is just being nosy, seeing what people buy and then going *beep, beep, beep* on that machine, but I don't want to know what the price is.

'Oh no!' Mum gasps and nearly drops the bags.

It's the price, isn't it? I KNEWED it. We didn't need the croissants or the ham. Why didn't we just get porridge and be done with it?

'Mollie?' Dad says. 'What's wrong, love?'

'Mum, is it because we got nice expensive food?'

'No . . . no . . . it's not that,' Mum says. 'It's *that* . . .'

And on the wall of the supermarket, with all the adverts and notices and deal offers is a poster saying:

MISSING

MUCH-LOVED CAT

GREY AND SILVER

FROM SOUTH LONDON AREA

And above that is a photograph of a cat, and we know *exactly* where that cat is.

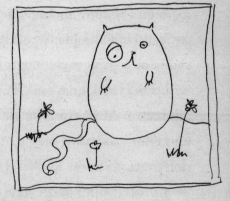

Asleep on our sofa.

'Mum! That's our Pork!' Poppy says.

'No, it can't be,' I argue. 'It must be another grey one.'

'It's Pork for sure,' Dad nods. Secretly he's happy, I bet, as him and Pork the cat have never seen eye to eye. Ever since Marnie and Donald Pincher found that homeless dollop and dropped him off at ours in that cardboard box in the middle of the night.

'It's him, look, the white on the tail, the wonky eye shape, the frown, the fat belly, the crooked ear,' Poppy says, and her eyes begin to water perfectly, as though a tincy pocket-sized watering can has taken the trouble of filling the wells of her eyes to the perfect level.

'I did always wonder how a stray could be that overweight,' Mum mutters to herself.

'Mum!' Poppy shouts. 'He's not overweight! He's perfect! He's absolutely perfect and he's *mine*.'

We all look at each other and then at the poster.

'I don't think he is ours, Pops. I think he belongs to this man' – Mum reads the poster – 'this man here . . . Giorgio . . . he has a phone number here too, look.'

'Forget about it, Mollie.' Dad crumples under the weight of Poppy's sad eyes – she sure loves that cat. 'Look, as far as we are concerned the cat was a stray. We housed it. He's ours now. That's his home, with us. We might never have even seen this poster if we weren't here today.'

'But we *have* seen it now,' Mum says. 'I'm writing the phone number down.'

'No . . . no . . . Mum . . . don't. Don't, please.' Poppy wraps her hands around Mum's fingers tightly, begging, but Mum looks away.

'I'm just writing it down, it doesn't mean I'll call,' Mum reassures, but Poppy is not convinced, as she knows that Mum is one real law-abiding citizen, so she starts to cry.

'Mollie, *don't*,' Dad argues firmly while giving in to Hector who needs a coin put into a slot in a machine just so that he can sit in this stupid baby car ride and go up and down for forty-five seconds while we hash this out. We begin to raise our voices in a squabble of arguing and disagreement, so much so that it has reached the point where nobody can hear the other think.

'Enough!' Mum screams. *Awwwwwwright, Mum, you didn't need to cause a scene.* 'Enough.' She scratches her head and we all go silent. 'This man . . . this Giorgio, he must be worried sick about his cat . . . Remember when we lost Lamb-Beth and how much our hearts hurt? Could you imagine if some family found her and selfishly didn't return her because they wanted her for themselves . . . not to even let us know that she was OK and alive and safe? Imagine how we would feel if that lovely lady from the allotment hadn't called up to say she had found her? How empty would we feel?'

We all look at our shoes. Mine have way too much mud on them for what is humanly acceptable for somebody that doesn't live 100% on a farm. I have no idea how my shoes got so grubby.

'OK. Let's call up the man,' Poppy mumbles, and then does a sniff, one of those sniffs to say *I COULD really have a good OLD massive MASSIVE cry over this at this moment but I'm choosing not to because I am growed up.* She is brave.

At home we are having tea from a pot like how Granny makes. Even though nobody says it, I can see our idealistic day of relaxation scampering briskly out the window, no thanks to this Giorgio bloke. Mum goes off to call him, the cat owner, but first Dad wants to check his messages.

'It's a Saturday, they won't call today,' Mum reassures him. 'Stop stressing,' she adds. But it only seems to make Dad crosserer. I think this is because he is a bit not working and mostly, as Dad says, 'playing the waiting game'. I would be AWFUL at that game.

Mum makes *the* call to Giorgio in the living room by the back doors that lead to the garden, so we can't hear her conversation. It's not that she's hiding anything – she just doesn't want to rub anything into our faces.

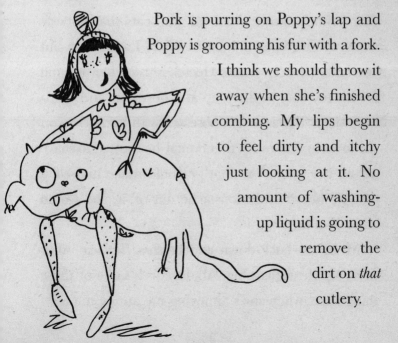

Pork is purring on Poppy's lap and Poppy is grooming his fur with a fork. I think we should throw it away when she's finished combing. My lips begin to feel dirty and itchy just looking at it. No amount of washing-up liquid is going to remove the dirt on *that* cutlery.

Mum walks back in.

'That was quick.' Dad looks up from his work.

'He didn't pick up the phone. But I left a message.'

'Phew,' I sigh deeply.

'Well, perhaps that's luck telling us we've done the right thing and hopefully he won't call back and things can remain as they are.' Mum tickles Pork's chin. 'Perhaps the poster was old,' she adds. Curse all the bits of paper that are hanging around at the moment. All they bring is bad news of sleepovers that nobody wants to attend, and cats that nobody wants to give back. I want to stroke Lamb-Beth but currently I can't because Hector is using her as a hill for his toy cars to drive up and down on and she is fast asleep. She is so SO obsessed with him. I reckon she loves him so much that even if he wanted to shave off all her fur just so that he could make himself a one-off beard and moustache out of it, she would allow him to.

Mum sits back down and finishes her tea. After every sip she sighs a big, 'Ah, lovely.' It's one of those things that when she's annoying me annoy me even more, but if she didn't do it my whole day would fall apart brick by brick.

'Ah, lovely,' she sighs again, and picks herself up to go and lie out on the sofa. A well-earned relax for Mum, I think.

Dad is getting · more and more stressed at the moment because he is taking all the responsibility for himself of us not having money. He thinks we don't know that he thinks we are going to get thrown onto the streets like tired old sad rag dolls and have to live inside a skip. What he doesn't realize is that I've thought ALL this through and the solution was simply right under his nostrils all along. He is a carpenter for his job. So when we get turfed from our house he can just build us a new street shack to live in. Right?

Anyway, when he's stressed he likes to clean. So now he leaps up and decides he wants to tidy the house all of a sudden, which, if I'm honest, always feels like he's trying to collect us and all our belongings, and throw *us* into a massive skip on the street. He starts with the kitchen, ruthlessly dashing away anything in his war path and hurdling stuff in the bin without looking twice. Pulling the toaster out and hoovering up the crumbs. It feels like the floor is getting lifted practically beneath my feet and gets slathered in thick eye-watering bleach. I'm not allowed to touch bleach because it is so dangerous and can burn your skin and make it go horrible and blistery so you mustn't be at all interested in it. I watch Dad scamper around, scrubbing and scraping and brushing and washing. He opens up the oven to clean inside and the skeleton of a blackened charcoal chip falls out and onto the floor. The oven is a thick deep dark black colour.

'Dis-gust-ing,' Dad spits, and gets to work on that, spraying and spritzing the entire oven with a moussey type foam. A browny-black sludge begins to drizzle out and never seems to stop coming. It's like a volcano. A volcano of lava poo. Splattering out in all these wretched colours and spilling down the sides.

'Can you get me a towel please?' he asks me.

'A towel?' I say, startled. I had sort of become quite happy watching the disgusting old oven juice oozing from the oven.

'Yes. A towel. That's what I just said, didn't I?'

Awwwwright, Dad. Calm it, Kermit. Jeeze, Louise. His temper is atrocious. 'Any towel, or . . .' I begin, but he snaps.

'Yes. *Any* towel. Any *towel. Any towel* will do. *A* towel will do,' he impatiently bites. Wow, *what's* the matter with him? It's probably because cleaning the oven is one of those jobs that once you start you have to finish, but once you start you completely regret even starting in the first place. With an old hand towel in my hand from the bathroom cupboard, I creep back into the kitchen, not wanting to annoy him any more than what I clearly already have done just simply by being alive.

'Here you go,' I say quietly.

'That's too small! That's never going to soak all this up,' he huffs, and points to the brown puddle of stinking mess on the floor that seems not to be getting any smaller.

'You said *any* towel,' I croak.

'Where's your initiative?' he snaps. 'Do I have to do EVERYTHING myself?' He now gets up and walks out, pinging his yellow rubber gloves off. He knows Mum would lose her marbles if he used a nice house towel. Besides, we don't have the money to go splish-sploshing about on fantastic fluffy new towels to replace the one he's going to use to mop up the oven vomit with. I decide I hate him right now.

Trudging back into the living room, I see Mum sprawled out on the couch with Poppy and Pork and Lamb-Beth and Hector all piled up on top of her. They are watching a baking competition. At the moment, this woman with a face like a Dorito chip is trying to make a picnic basket out of cake, and all the picnic stuff inside the basket is even made out of cake and icing: little sandwiches, a pot of jam, fruit and scones . . . *all* out of cake. The picnic basket, as it's made out of cake too, keeps collapsing and sticking to the things inside the basket, and the cake is too hot to decorate and the icing keeps sliding off, but because they are on a timer she can't wait any longer. The icing has turned to scrambled egg. The marzipan looks a mess but fun to play with. Everybody is gripped.

'Come and watch, monkey?' Mum leans her arms out to me. I see there isn't too much space for me on the sofa or on her body. Mum sometimes forgets that now I am more olderer and not a tiny little child baby doll any more that can just lie on top of her chest and weigh the same as a satsuma. I can't squeeze my big bum in the shopping trolley any more, and my feet touch the floor now when I sit on the sofa rather than just poking off the edge like Hector's. But after how Dad's being . . . I just can't resist.

With all my body weight, which I have crisps and chips and bacon and cookies and cheese to thank for, I lie on top of my mum and let her let me think I am the smallest little bunny rabbit in the world and that all I need is kisses and cuddles and love and love and love and love and love when really I am a huge mammoth beast.

I smell my mum. That one smell that is the one I know. The smell that lets me know why the words *fam*iliar and *fam*ily begin the same: FAM. It smells of warm and washing powder and wine and straw-berries and pears and roses and I a bit let a tear come, but for no reason because I am not really that sad, and I just let it go. Like a firework that explodes for no one to watch. It softly dribbles down my nose and into my mouth and it tastes of heated salt and then it a bit hits her chest, but she doesn't bring it up and just kisses my head and continues to watch the desperate Dorito-faced woman turn some more Victoria sponge into a basket.

Then Mum sort of says to us all in a calmly voice, 'Dad's really stressed at the moment, OK? Basically, he went for an interview, a big interview, to renovate a whole entire brand-new toy shop and he hasn't heard back and he doesn't know if he's got it or not!'

'A toy shop?' Hector's eyes go wild.

'WOW!' Poppy giggles.

'Keep it down, he is really nervous about it, he doesn't think he's got it and he really wants it, and because he hasn't heard back he can't take on any more work.'

'That would be AMAZING!' I want to jump up and down but I have to hide it all in.

'He hasn't told you guys because he doesn't want to disappoint you if he doesn't get it, but I wanted to tell you, in case he's a bit snappy. OK? So keep quiet about it, but if he shouts or is short-tempered with you, it's not your fault, OK? You have to take everything with a pinch of salt.'

'What's a pinch of salt?' Hector asks.

'You know what a pinch of salt is,' Mum says back.

'It's a pinch.' Poppy then pinches Hector's arm and he yells and smacks her in the eye. I am well jealoused that he got the chance to do that as I would give anything to openly smack Poppy in the eye socket. We all wait for Poppy to laugh or cry, but she does neither.

'Yeah . . . actually, what *does* a pinch of salt mean?' she then asks.

'It means . . . everything he says, pretend you have a little pinch of salt to swallow it down with . . . basically . . . don't take him too seriously. Don't take his words to heart,' Mum fills us in, and then goes back to watching the cake basket being built on TV.

'I want to take Dad with a piece of chocolate,' Hector says.

'Yes, does that mean then that every time Dad is a horror that we get a piece of chocolate?'

Mum laughs at this. 'No, it does not. But you can say it if you like . . . if it makes it easier.'

I hope Dad does get that job. Then maybe perhaps I can just go in there all the time and look at all the things my dad made with even his own hands. Maybe I can buy a toy from there. A growed up one, obviously, but I don't ever want to be a growed-up human with terrible brain-eating issues like money and work and war and taxes and coffee and passports and banks and scary forms and DIY and hangovers . . . which is when you go to one too many parties and then wake up the next morning only to find to your absolute horror that your brain has tipped upside down.

'He will be back to normal soon, I promise. Everything will be OK.'

'Darcy?' Dad calls me into the kitchen. I get a bit nervoused. What if it's time for more telling off or if the sludge from the oven has doubled in size and is now an ocean of black and brown grime? 'Darcy, come here a sec?' he calls again.

'Go on,' Mum says. 'Go and see what Dad wants.'

'OK.' I get up and enter the kitchen. The afternoon sun is falling away and is throwing a beautiful pink and orange shade into the kitchen. The light is warming. Dad is standing by the sink directly in front of the window.

'Come here . . .' He invites me to join him up by the sink. 'OK, now just stand here and close your eyes.'

'What, here? In front of the window?'

'Yes.'

'It's so sunny,' I laugh.

'Close your eyes,' he says, and I look at him and he's got his eyes closed too so I shut mine all crinkled shut. The sun is reaching all over our faces and it feels so lovely. 'I'm holding a bucket of cleaning bleach,' he laughs, 'and when you face the sun, with the bleach, you can almost mistake the smell for chlorine, you know, what they clean the swimming pools with? And it feels like you're on holiday . . . you know, in a hot country, by the pool? The sun on your face. On a sun lounger. Your mum would be next to me, you, Poppy and Hector. A beer, a good book . . . no worries whatsoever. Wouldn't that be nice?'

'Yes, that would be.' I laugh some more. It does feel like we're on holiday, for a small moment. The moment before we realize how totally weird we are, standing by the window withour eyes closed, gripping onto a bucket of bleach just to pretend we are on holiday, just to pretend we have no worries and so I say to

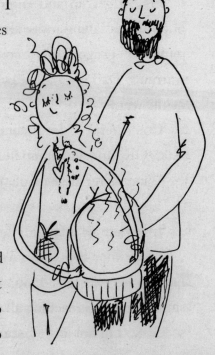

96

him what I think I should say, something that Mum just said to me . . . 'Everything will be OK.'

And he grips my hand and quickly tips the bleach down the sink. We haven't had a holiday in ages.

But everything is NOT OK.

After we have all gone to bed, after Dad's cleaning and the woman on the TV show gets knocked out of the baking competition, when the house is a bleachy-smelling dream of cleanliness and quietness, the phone rings in the middle of the night.

I sit bolt upright in pure fear and not knowing what to do with myself in panic, but then Dad is croakily grumbling and I cock my head into the door to listen as much as what I can. I then hear Mum's footsteps and then Poppy's door creak-cracks open in the darkness. Her lime-green night lamp floods alien shine into the hallway and it sneaks under the gap in my door, as if a UFO has just landed outside my bedroom.

I snap the door open. Poppy is already on the landing. Then Mum's voice begins grumbling away too, and I'm confused and trying so much to guess what is going on but I can't hear or understand anything. And Dad has his hands in his hair and is looking worried and Mum is sitting on the stairs still on the phone. I look at Poppy, who winks at me. She is wearing MY jellybean nightie, that used to be my favourite one but now I'm too big for it, and it makes me livid every time I see her in it. I'm too afraid to even lean onto the banister like she does in case my grotesque self smashes it and I fall down the stairs.

'Do you think that *Pork* is the cat's real name? Is it time?' She looks worried. 'Are they coming to get him and take him away?' she whispers at me from across the hall, and I feel terribly nervous that that's the truth. But would that Giorgio man *really* call to reclaim his missing cat in the middle of the night? I mean, I know it's his pet and everything, but surely he could wait until the morning. And I know it's late because even Mum and Dad were in bed.

'I don't know. Let's wait until Mum's off the phone,' I whisper back and try to listen and hear more.

Mum is speaking quietly into the phone and being all worried and dry-throated, and Dad is now pacing which is making me nervous still more. Mum begins to cry softly a bit, but I know this only because her voice is cracking and dry and breaking. Poppy and I are still guessing, and then when we can't stand to listen to our amazing Mum's tears any more we gently go and sit down next to her on the stairs and try our very best to creep and not crash and bang, and then we squidgy in our bums next to and around her and she grips us tightly and then talks some more and a bit more, still crying and a bit more, and then gets off the phone and with big red wet eyes says very gently:

'Granny, my mum, your granny . . . has died.'

Chapter Six

I didn't feel sad. And I didn't know why.

I tried really hard to remember all the things I liked about Granny. Which, to be realistic, weren't many, but it was still awful. I even tried to remember my little trick which was to remember how she cared for my mum but it didn't make me cry. I thought about how I wasn't going to see her ever again. That the last time I saw her I was thinking how her mouth looked like a dog's bum and that was our final goodbye and how we didn't even know that.

The guilt from not being sad made me feel cross at myself.

I was thinking of what to say to Mum. How to make her feel betterer, but I didn't know what to say. Or where to start. Her mum had just dropped off the edge of Planet Life and I couldn't even squeeze a tear out. I was a terrible human being.

I slept so well too. Not even feeling one bit upsetted. Guilt. Everywhere. Suffocated me.

Before I went downstairs for breakfast I went to the bathroom and brushed my teeth with the cheap budget toothpaste. I needed a new toothbrush by the looks of things, but it wasn't a good time I guess to go demanding a toiletry supply.

I faced the mirror.

Squeeze some tears out, Darcy. Come on. One will do.

I focused. Hard. I looked into my own eyes. The colours, the lines, the shades. The big black hole in the middle. Weird. Why is there a big black hole in my eye?

I'm losing concentration.

I try again.

I pretend I am winning an Oscar. That usually makes me cry. During my acceptance speech. I gasp,

'Thank you, thank you, thank you.'

No tears, dry as a bone.

I try and force them out. Like doing a poo.

Nothing.

I gently put my hands under the tap. It doesn't make realistic tears to just wet your face – you have to gently wet your finger and drip it out the corner of your eye. So that it slides down. My sleeves get all wet. There isn't much worse things than a wet sleeve.

Oh, why did Granny have to die anyway? Well. At least it wasn't my best grandma. The one I truly love.

Oh, I feel guilty again now.

This is torture.

I poke myself in my eye. I want to get the big black circle in the centre, but my eye keeps on shutting every time my finger gets close.

I decide to stare my eyes open. Nice and big. The dryness will make my eyeballs naturally cry all by themselves.

There we go.

A single salty tear dribbles quietly down my cheek.

Pathetic.

If I'm quick enough I can show it off to Mum and be like, 'Look, Mum, here is a tear, look, it's for you.' But it dries up much quicker than it fell and I doubt I have the energy to produce another.

I am the worst granddaughter in the world.

Well. Anyway. *She* was the worst granny in the world.

So that makes two of us.

The only thing we had in common was that we had nothing in common.

I give up on the crying and leave the bathroom. Poppy walks past.

'Eugh!' She crinkles her face up in disgust.

'What?'

'You're not *crying*, are you?'

'No. I was pretending.'

'Why?'

'Because Granny's dead.'

'Oh, yeah. I forgot.'

OK. So maybe I'm NOT the worst.

'Can you teach me how to cry like that?' she asks before we head downstairs.

'Why?'

'It's just a useful technique.'

'Yeah, but you'll use it against me. You'll start fake crying one day when we have a fight or something.'

'Keep your friends close but your enemies *closer*, Darcy.' Poppy winks. She has been doing drama club after school and you can SO tell.

I'm starving. I fancy crumpets. Slathered in butter and Marmite. I love the way that when you bite into a crumpet the inside looks like a forest of corridors. I am going to EAT!

Are you allowed to enjoy food when someone's dead?

Are you allowed to enjoy *anything*?

When we get into the kitchen it is silent. Like someone has died. Oh yeah. They did.

Mum is pottering about. Being a waif.

'Morning, Mum, are you OK?'

'Yes,' she says all weirdly, 'I'm as right as rain.'

Rain never seemed right to me.

Mum always told me if I ever found myself in an awkward environment then I should just make myself

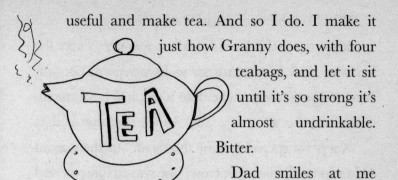

useful and make tea. And so I do. I make it just how Granny does, with four teabags, and let it sit until it's so strong it's almost undrinkable. Bitter.

Dad smiles at me gently and helps us do breakfast. At least he looks cheerier.

I was worried about Mum's emotions. But she seems to be fine. She makes some phone calls for a bit and just wants to spend all day in the garden digging and planting with the radio blabbering in the background, which is fine by me.

'Is Mum OK?' I ask Dad as we clear away the breakfast crumbs. Sometimes Poppy, Hector and I eat like a bunch of wild hyenas that have never seed food before and we eat so quickly it's like we can't even remember doing it. Inhaling it in one breath.

'I think so, monkey. It's just a shock, isn't it? It was so sudden, and they had a funny relationship, didn't they?'

'Why? Is it because Mum's adopted?'

'No, I don't think so. I think it was very lucky for her and your Uncle Adrian to be adopted, but you know what Granny is like. She is . . . *was* . . . I mean, quite *set in her ways* . . . what I mean by that is that . . . sorry for speaking ill of the dead, but she was an old-fashioned miserable crow! She was so difficult and always complaining. It annoyed her that your mum moved to London to live with me, and your uncle moved to New York. She didn't realize that by being so controlling, once they were old enough, they left her anyway.'

'If she was nice to them, they might have stayed with her.'

'They might have.'

'How did she die?' I ask. I lick the knife of its remaining peanut butter.

'She was old. She died peacefully. In her sleep. She had been ill on and off for a while. Still a shock though, right? So suddenly like that!'

'Or maybe it was a week babysitting us that did it!' A dark grin forms over my face.

Dad laughs. 'Probably! The final straw! I'll be next!' he jokes, which is naughty but true.

Maybe we did kill Granny. By being just too fun?

'Go out and speak to your mum,' Dad suggests. 'Here, take her this cup of tea.'

I carry the hot mug carefully, concentrating not to spill it or tip it, out into the garden.

'Why are you planting all those twiggy stick leaf things?' I ask her, pointing at the bundle of basically twiggy stick leaf things.

'These are herbs.' Mum smiles at me, reaching for the tea. Her glasses have splatters of wet earth on them. 'This is rosemary, this is thyme . . . smell them.'

I smudge the green branch between my fingers; it's so strong. 'Smells like when people cook up lamb!' I shout. 'I hate it!' I NEVER eat lamb because of precious Lamb-Beth.

'No, that's because people often cook lamb with

rosemary, but not us. It tastes delicious on roast potatoes too.'

'OK,' I grumble.

'My mum, your granny, when she was alive, used to take all the herbs and make bouquet garnis and hand them out to the neighbours.'

'What's a bou-ket-blah-gardening?'

'*Bouquet garni* is when you take a little branch of each herb and tie them together with string, like a little bouquet of flowers, and then drop them into your stew or soup. You tie them together so once you've cooked the food you can easily locate the bunch of herbs, as nobody wants to eat sticks.'

'Nobody wants to eat string either.'

'Yes, well that's why you take them out at the end.'

'Can we make bouquet garnis?'

'Of course. I'll bring some herbs in when I'm done here.'

'They'll make good flowers for Poppy's dolls to get married with. They can hold them in their arms . . . it will be so realistic . . .'

'You could slip a few daisies in there too!' Mum smiles.

I smile back. But then the wind passes and little dots snake-sneak up my arms like I've been pricked by a zillion crazy needles and my hairs stand on end and my eyes water. I run back inside. The cold doesn't seem to bother Mum today.

Watching Mum from the kitchen window, I wash up the teapot and I start to daydream. I begin to write in my head. I can see the words forming, letter by letter . . . line by line . . .

A bit one of my dreams is to be like a girl that lived a few hundred years ago and maybe be a servant girl or something. I would like to wear one of those bandana-type headscarves wrapped around my head and a long skirt with an apron. I would want to wear long knitted socks and boots with buttons *and* laces that clip-clop so much when I walk down any cobbled street or pavement.

My name would be a flower name, but not Poppy . . . like Rosie or something. Rosie doesn't much like being a servant but for one reason or another she just doesn't have one single choice because . . . well, *because*, and she must not complain because all the best characters that have to suffer like that never complain because it makes the reader not like them as much if they do.

Rosie is adopted by this family but they are not a very good adopted family because they make Rosie be a servant girl. They are posh and she is not. The house she works in is next door to an orphanage. Her jobs include things like:

– sweeping with a Cinderella-type broom (like not a normal broom – it has to be made from a branch of tree and look really old-fashioned)

– making and *poking* the fire but not with her finger, with a tong and maybe using one of those big billow things to make the fire roar morer

– carrying pails of water up huge hills on one of those long stick things with rope and a bucket at either end that's made out of rickety wood and the water sloshes about so much

– ironing, even though she is young and not allowed yet. And it's an iron without a wire, like a really heavy industrial just all-metal one that sometimes 'scalds' her hand

– scrubbing the floor with one of those bristle brushes and she has to use two hands and be on her knees

– 'draw' (run, basically) the wretched lady of the house a bath and then wash the wretched lady's back with a sponge

– and make meat and vegetable stews in big metal pots using bouquet garnis for flavour.

Aside from being a servant, Rosie is absolutely terrific at being a witch doctor. But it is her secret. In her little room under the stairs, in the basement, she has very quietly mastered the skill of brewing up some fantastic formulas and medicines. She has remedies for most things,

and all are made from natural things like
flowers and plants and herbs, and spices from
extracts of things that sound really important
like *Milk Thistle* and *Cowslip* and *Marigold*,
and even liquorice but not ever the sweetie one.

Rosie has only time for five hours' sleep
each night in her uncomfortable iron bed with
all the springs poking out, because her chores
are so never-ending and two of her hours she
must spend creating and working on her mixtures
and potions. She must practise and get better if
she is to be a true witch doctor, but it is so
hard because she is so tired and hungry from a
day's work that all she can do is eat her cold
gruel and hard stale bread crust and cheese for
dinner and fall asleep. Sometimes she has other
chores to do, like patch up her servant costumes
and relace her boots, or do some extra stitching
for the house, and all this must be done by
candlelight. Often her brewing and cooking of
medicines and potions come last.

But there is a strange bug going around.

> A new child has come into the orphanage and with him has come a nasty bug. It is a horrid disease that makes you be sick and poo and sneeze at the same time. If you get it you need to be near two toilets so you can . . .

'Hector?' Hector is dipping cheese-and-onion crisps into chocolate spread right now.

'Yeah?' He looks at me. He has brown all around his mouth from the chocolate.

'It looks like you have lipstick on.'

'Lick stick?'

'Whatever. Right, I have a question for you . . .'

'Yeah?'

'Would you rather be sick all day, poo all day or sneeze all day?'

'Oh, that's easy,' Hector replies. 'Poo. I LOVE poo.'

Gross.

I think I need to do *something* with myself. I focus

on putting glitter, my favourite colour, on my nails, which I did worry was slightly inappropriate given that Granny had just died, but Mum was outside so she couldn't smell it and anyway it was too late now – the glitter was on and you know what *they* say about glittery nail varnish: 'Once it's on, it's on.' They don't say that, but they should. It's true, after all. Whoever *they* are.

'I want nails like that,' Hector said, and so I obliged, after making him wash the disgusting chocolate spread out of his nails. I paint them blue and glittery, just like mines. He wasn't very good at sitting still.

I said, 'You aren't very good at sitting still, are you?' To which he lifted his finger up and shoved it right up his nose to begin searching for bogey nuggets, completely covering the cave of his nostril in blue glitter. I gave up.

'I'm hungry.' Poppy trudged in, even though she had only just eaten, saying it over and over like a record that was spinning round and round, but me too to be perfectly Frank (I STILL don't know who this Frank guy is, by the way) and then the phone rang.

We are scared to answer the phone these days; it's only ever bad news or bad news. Dad looked fearful. Perhaps it was the toy shop calling and they were about to yell, 'YES, MATE, YOU DID IT! YOU'VE GOT THE JOB!' But we couldn't show we knew he was waiting so we had to pretend we didn't care.

'I'll get it!' Poppy chimed.

'It will only be for you anyway, Popsicle, I'm sure!' Dad politely joked as Poppy's social circle is ever growing like an apple orchard in full bloom. Meanwhile, mine is like a desert with one solitary cactus in the centre. The cactus being Will.

Dad began to try and make early lunch on Poppy's request, quickly realizing that our shopping trip at the supermarket yesterday only consisted of comfortable immediate snack food to eat there and then and nothing substantial. He began rooting through the cupboards. *Pickled onion, digestive biscuit and cat food sandwiches, anyone?*

Reason number 167453 of why you shouldn't go food shopping when you're hungry.

Poppy, as if she hadn't ever even answered a phone call, daintily stepped back into the kitchen and began humming in that 'NOTHING going on here, guys' type way, which incidentally screams *PAY ATTENTION TO ME!*

'Who was that?' I ask. Dad tried not to care. Well done, Daddio.

'Mind your own beeswax.' She bats me away and starts rummaging through the crisps drawer. *Uh-huh, babes*, you heard correctly, we do have a WHOLE

116

drawer dedicated to the mighty joy that is crisps. Except at the moment it's just the rubbish cheapo brand that taste like salted cardboard. Still, a crisp is a crisp. It's all joy.

'Poppy, who was it?' Dad asks, concerned now. Come on, Pops. Put Dad out of his misery.

'Nobody.' She chooses ready salted, which instantly lets me know something is *up*. She was distracted and completely bypassed the prawn cocktail, the cheese and onion, the smoky bacon.

'Tell!' I say.

'NO!' she screams back all loud and screechy out of nowhere.

'Calm down, Poppy, no need for shouting.'

'Yeah, Poppy.'

'Stay out of my business,' she hisses, and then adds, 'Just because you're a writer doesn't mean you get to spy in on my whole entire life.' And then she walks out. Crunching her crisps and being a *terrible*.

Dad and I don't need even to take two looks at each other before we completely know exactly who was on the other end of the phone. We know, because

117

if there's one thing Poppy loves doing, it's being on the phone and that phone call lasted all of 1.5 seconds, and if there's a second thing Poppy loves doing, it's re-telling all of us the conversations she had on the phone, and she is trying to pretend that this phone call didn't happen at all.

Leaving really only one likely candidate.

Giorgio. Pork's *real* dad.

'I'll call him back,' Dad says.

Chapter Seven

I can't stand the sadness or the weirdness that is pressing its big ugly foot on our home. How Mum and Dad are worrying about money and our granny has only just gone and died, but it seems even sadderer that there is a highly likely chance that Pork is leaving us. I feel odd and guilty about that but Mum won't let us feel bad. In truth, I don't think it matters what others think about how you actually feel because only you know what somebody meant to you. And yes, personally I knowed Pork more than what I knewed my granny and what I knewed of her I didn't even really understand or like even so much.

Sometimes you just can't feel bad about something that is out of your control. Like once a blister on my heel popped and blister juice dripped onto and bledded on Henrietta from next-door's white couch and she wasn't mad at me because it was out of my control. She knew that I didn't want popped blister blooding everywhere no more than what she wanted blister juice sponging up on the couch. I wonder what kind of guy this Giorgio is . . . What if Giorgio is not a nice man? Is he the kind of bloke that would go ballistic if somebody's blister blooded on his couch or not? What if he's a horror?

I humph upstairs and peel open my writing book, I want to write about Rosie and what she will do next with the bouquet garnis and the orphanage, but then another idea starts tinkling in my head, like a little gold bell ringing 'choose me, choose me instead . . .' I can hear the radio from downstairs playing softly music and so I start to write something completely new . . .

Butter would not melt in the mouth of Mrs
Tulip Sandtails. (Oh, SORRY about me and my

terminology of new phrases.) You would always find her pottering in the garden, trimming the ripe red roses back, choosing the best sprigs of rosemary, thyme and bay leaf to make mini bouquet garnis to give to her neighbours for their dinner. She was always waving 'hello' and telling people the time from her little brown leather strap watch. You would often see her wearing a huge duck-egg blue bonnet and frilly skirt, tinkling the bell on her

squeaky wheeled bicycle, her basket full to the brim of fresh bread and sweeties for the children.

Mrs Tulip Sandtails ADORED cats and just had to stop by and stroke the chins of any she passed while out on her errands. She had even been known to sew and knit little outfits for the local cats and kittens in her village; she was thoughtful like that. Any cat she met, she loved it. They were her true weakness.

If she ever saw anybody sitting in the sun with their cat she would have to pull over on her bicycle and go to them.

'If there was one thing I would love . . . it would be to have a cat of my own, to love and care for,' she would say, gripping her kitten-embroidered hand-stitched handkerchief close to her chest.

'Why don't you get a cat?' the people often asked her.

'Alas, I cannot,' she muttered. 'I have an allergy to them.' And then she would let out a perfectly timed splash of a sneeze. 'Bless me,' she would add, sniffling.

'Poor you,' the person who she was in

conversation with would normally reply.

She would try not to cry, holding the tears back. 'Of all the people to suffer from such a nasty allergy, it *couldn't* have happened to a bigger animal-lover.'

'Or a *nicer* person,' that person would usually say, or something along the lines of that.

'Oh, stop it,' Mrs Tulip Sandtails would shriek. 'You're too kind,' she would say, and then she would stroke the cat one last time. 'I know I'm not meant to stroke or pet them because of my allergy, but I just can't resist their beautiful fur, their perky ears, their whiskers and tails.' Mrs Tulip Sandtails' hand would quiver at just the touch of them, her reaction was quite severe.

'Yes, they are quite special,' the person might add.

'But my favourite bit about a cat is the lips.' Mrs Tulip Sandtails closed her eyes in pride.

'The lips?'

'Yes. I just adore cats' lips, don't you?'

'I hadn't really noticed their lips — do they have lips?'

'Oh yes!' she would say and sometimes, if she was feeling comfortable with the person, Mrs Tulip Sandtails would lift the cat's jaw to show the person the lips of the cat. 'See?'

'Of course, I can't believe I missed the cat's lips all along! Silly me!'

'You should pay closer attention to your cat, my friend.' Mrs Tulip Sandtails would smile. 'You never know when somebody could just take it away from you.' Her eyes dazzled. 'Listen to me,' she tutted, 'not that that would *ever* happen in a lovely friendly village like this.' And then she would totter off, clamber back onto her bicycle and ride away, calling, 'Toodleoo . . .'

The allergy was frustrating for Mrs Tulip Sandtails, and people in the village really felt sorry for her. Imagine being such a lovely and thoughtful kind lady and having such a dreadful

disease: an allergy to your favourite thing –
could you imagine? Think of your favourite
thing . . .

Mine is writing and Maltesers and fried egg
and chips and Lamb-Beth. Imagine if I was
allergic to those things!

Mrs Tulip Sandtails did so much for the
community too; she ran the CPS (the Cat
Protection Society), she 'adopted' several cats
from all over the world, gave money to 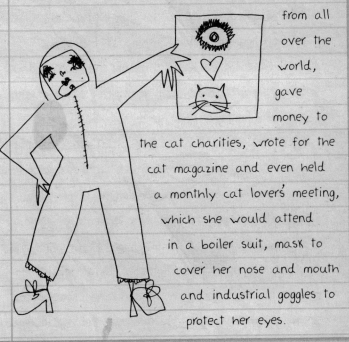 the cat charities, wrote for the
cat magazine and even held
a monthly cat lover's meeting,
which she would attend
in a boiler suit, mask to
cover her nose and mouth
and industrial goggles to
protect her eyes.

'She is the most selfless person I've ever met!' the people would say.

'She is so generous and loving, I aspire to be like her,' they may even add.

'If only I could put our four-legged furry friends on top of *my* priority list,' they might even be tempted to say. 'Sometimes I think *I've* got it bad, and then I realize how lucky and fortunate I truly am.'

One night, during a terrible arrival of some extreme thunder and lightning, a little boy named Wallace was sitting on the park bench in his usual yellow rain mac. He liked to let the rain pellet on his head. Wallace's dad never bothered to ask where Wallace was going when he left on these evenings in the rain, he never asked when he was coming home either, he just sort of . . . let him leave. If Wallace ever stayed out really late, which he often did, Wallace's dad never bothered to go looking for him. I didn't really have an exact answer to why he didn't care. But neither did Wallace.

126

His dad just didn't care.

On these evenings, Wallace would stroll through the graveyard with his pet, Amigo, a homeless dog. Amigo wasn't allowed to live with Wallace and his dad because Wallace's dad hated animals. EVEN Amigo. When he saw him, it would just make Wallace's dad even more angrier at the world than what he already was. So Amigo lived in the graveyard, where he would just hang and chill with the stones and souls. It wasn't a scary graveyard. I understand some are, but this one wasn't. It was where Wallace's granny had been buried and he knew it well. Before she died, they used to take walks around it, for the peace and quiet.

Wallace could not find Amigo tonight. He was tired of looking and was slumped on the park bench, depressed and unhappy. *Where had Amigo gone?* It was unlike him to go disappearing, particularly on a night like this, with thunder and lightning, which was his favourite! They always had such fun in the bad weather.

Wallace had searched everywhere. It wasn't much fun for Wallace being out in the rain without Amigo. There was nobody to chase him or for him to chase back. Nobody to dig bones up with, nobody to howl at the moon with or raid the dustbins with, where Wallace might find the odd chocolate bar and Amigo could find a delicious dirty nappy to devour. And so eventually, he wandered home, back to his little poky bedroom, with the rain smacking him on the shoulders.

'Wallace! Wallace!' His dad's shout woke him. It wasn't a good shout or a bad shout, it was just a sort of shout. But it didn't happen very often. To be honest, it surprised Wallace that his father even knew his name. 'There's

someone at the door for you, some happy lady
that smells of strawberries and flowers . . .'

'What?' Wallace was shocked. Nobody ever
came to the door for him.

'It better not be a teacher,' his dad
mumbled. 'You had better not been misbehaving,'
his dad muttered, without even looking him in
the eye.

And there at the door was Mrs Tulip
Sandtails.

She was a shortish lady. Not as young as
Mum is, but not as old as Granny was before
she died. She had curly brown reddy hair and
shiny eyes and pink glossy lipstick on and fluffy
rabbit-like whiskers nestled on her top lip. Dad
was right, Wallace thought — she did smell of
fruit and flowers. She wore a matching jacket
and skirt covered in little illustrations of tigers
and shiny purple shoes. She took one of her
white driving gloves off and put her hand
forward for Wallace to shake.

'Are you Wallace?' She smiled; her white

teeth sparkled in the new spring morning.

'Yes. How do you know who I am?'

'I don't mean to startle you; firstly, I know most people, or at *least* the faces in the community. I am on the council, the advisory panel for the mayor and well . . . I never shy from a friendly face . . . but also . . . I found this . . .'

Mrs Tulip Sandtails handed Wallace the beaten-up bootlace that Wallace had tied around Amigo's neck as a collar. Amigo had worn it for years. Wallace had even made a little tag around his neck with his and Amigo's name on it, and it had Wallace's address etched into the back.

Wallace felt as though somebody had shoved a hand down his throat and wrapped their hand around his heart and was squeezing. It was a bittersweet feeling. Sweet that Amigo's collar had been found . . . but bitter that Amigo wasn't wearing it.

'Oh . . . and I found something else too!'

Mrs Tulip Sandtails smiled grandly as Amigo bounded up to Wallace and began sniffing and licking his face for ever. Wallace giggled hysterically.

'You must have been so worried,' Mrs Tulip Sandtails soothed. 'He must be happy to be home.'

'Kind of, but this isn't his home. My dad won't allow it.'

Mrs Tulip Sandtails clutched her throat. 'So where does Amigo live?' she asked, her eyelashes fluttering.

'Nowhere. Well . . . mostly he sleeps in the graveyard.'

'No wonder he went missing.'

This made Wallace feel sad and worried. 'I know. It's wrong. But he's my only friend.'

'I would say he could live at mine, but I am furiously allergic to animals.'

'So is my dad,' Wallace grunted.

'And anyway, I'm much more a cat person. If I had to choose.'

To that Amigo barked at the
thin air, rolled over and
pushed his bum up
and dropped a
gigantic cloud
of stagnant fart
into the air.

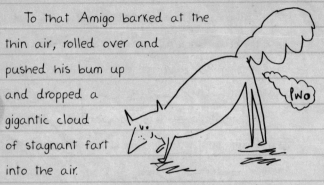

Mrs Tulip Sandtails laughed politely. 'I
don't think Amigo agrees. But I can see he
is a happy dog. Some dogs have everything,
thousands of pounds spent on their food and
beddings and toys that they only chew up . . .
not to mention the veterinary bills alone . . .
and they are not happy at all. This dog has
nothing — but look how his happiness beams off
him. It is a delight to see.'

This made Wallace feel better. He was so
happy to have his Amigo back.

'I live just on the other side of the park,
number sixty-four, with the white fence and
the brass cat doorknocker. Do come by for tea
one day.'

'I will.' Wallace waved back.

Mrs Tulip Sandtails stroked underneath Amigo's chin, and Amigo growled.

'Amigo!' Wallace scolded the dog. 'That's not nice. Mrs Sandtails is the one that found you, so be nice.'

But Amigo ducked his head.

Mrs Tulip Sandtails did not seem offended, and if she was she did a very good job of hiding it. 'Cheerio,' she called. Wallace had never heard anybody in his whole history of being alive say *cheerio* in actual real life. But he liked it.

The next evening came as soon as the moon popped up, followed by more thunder and lightning. Wallace and Amigo were weaving in between gravestones, mazing their way through the brambles and knots of thorns. Amigo stopped dead in his tracks and began to bark.

'What is it, Amigo?' Wallace ran over to see what had made him stop.

A tiny cry could be heard from the bushes.

It was a kitten. She was a very cute kitten. She was tiny and grey, not much bigger than a mug, with pink ears and a pink nose. Her fur was so soft that when it touched your skin it felt like a cloud was kissing you. Her eyes were apple green and were big and bug-eyed. She was shaking, terrified, her little tail propped up. Wallace gulped at her cuteness. He couldn't leave her here.

Wallace let the cat-shaped doorknocker clatter on number 64. It was late and the rain was still smashing down. The kitten was inside Wallace's pocket; her heart was beating so quickly. Amigo kept nuzzling her, trying to keep her warm and he didn't even LIKE cats. It was late. Mrs Tulip Sandtails may not answer at this hour, Wallace thought.

But she did.

'Wallace!' she cried. 'What a lovely surprise,

I wasn't expecting you . . . come inside.' Mrs Tulip Sandtails stood in a fluffy pastel dressing gown and silk lilac slippers. She opened the door right away, letting Wallace and Amigo have a great look inside. The bright orange light surrounding her from her house made it seem warm and inviting, comforting and cosy. 'Don't get any wetter, please do come inside.'

And so they did.

Wallace knew she was allergic, but he was pretty certain that once the *lovely* Mrs Tulip Sandtails saw the adorable little kitten, her heart would break. Besides, he had no other options – he couldn't take the kitten back home with him. Not with Dad.

Wallace stepped inside Mrs Tulip Sandtails' house but Amigo didn't seem as certain. He reluctantly forced his legs into the floor outside, as though his feet were setting in wet cement.

'Come on, boy.' Wallace pulled Amigo by the collar.

'Poor thing, every house probably scares him

if he's been homeless for so long,' Mrs Tulip Sandtails cooed at Amigo. Although it was clear Amigo did not want to go inside, he wanted to be with Wallace more and so, with his head hung low, he padded into the house behind his best friend.

Despite the lateness of the evening, Mrs Tulip Sandtails made honey on bread served on china plates that were decorated in cat heads and warm milk served in cat-shaped saucers. The walls were splattered in cat artwork, portraits of kittens and cats, statues and ornaments.

Wallace smiled politely, but all the while he could feel the tiny heartbeat of the baby cat in his pocket. He just had to wait for the right moment to bring it out. Mrs Tulip Sandtails seemed so happy to see them both and it had been such a long while since Amigo had eaten anything as delicious or felt the warm snug of a radiator, he didn't want to spoil it.

Wallace decided to ask Mrs Tulip Sandtails about her allergy, to keep her busy while Amigo wolfed down his third round of honey on bread.

'It must be tough for you to . . . you know . . . have a nasty cat allergy when you love cats so much.' Wallace bit into the honey on bread. It fell apart in toasty comforting loveliness. It was so buttery and sweet.

'Total nightmare.'

'How bad is your allergy, then?'

'Oh, terrible.' Mrs Tulip Sandtails pitied herself, pulling her warm cup of milk in close to her chest. 'It's got so bad that a cat just has to be close and the smell of one alone can make me collapse!'

Wallace choked on his milk. Amigo pretended not to hear and continued to lick the honey off his bread.

'Really?' Wallace's voice scratched.

'Oh, entirely, it's got *so* bad that if a cat was to ever even set foot in my house, I would come up in black and blue and purple pimples and my eyes would dry out and roll out of my skull.'

Wallace gently put his hand into his pocket and stroked the kitten softly.

'So you would never have a kitten as a pet?'

'Of course not! I would die a trillion times over.' Mrs Tulip Sandtails chimed breezily, 'More milk?'

Wallace suddenly had a quiet moment of thought to himself. If she *was* as allergic as she said she was, how come she had *not* reacted to the kitten in his pocket for all the time that Wallace and Amigo had been there? There was no collapsing going on, or black, blue and purple pimples and certainly no eyeball rolling! So why didn't she want a cat if she wasn't allergic? Why make up such an obscure lie?

He got the confidence to reach into his pocket and pull out the kitten and said very quickly, 'Look, Mrs Tulip Sandtails, I know you are allergic but I know you would take great care of this kitten, if you would just—'

'Get that thing out of my house!' Mrs Tulip Sandtails roared. Her eyes almost changed colour into a deep fiery orange glow as she snarled, 'NOW!'

'No, wait, honestly . . . Mrs Tulip Sandtails . . . if you would just . . . see how cute she is . . . please . . . she was shivering in the graveyard, we didn't know where else to take her . . . we just knew you loved cats and . . .'

Mrs Tulip Sandtails began to get hotter and hotter, her blood began to boil, she began to get so hot she was turning orange. The kitten began to cry and her fur stood on end. Amigo began to shiver and shake himself, and he growled and howled. Mrs Tulip Sandtails began to erupt, more and more. She started to hiss and then, suddenly, began to grow. She was splitting out of her clothes! Her pastel dressing gown started to shred, her silk slippers popped off her feet, and out of her toes big black claws began to appear, and the same happened from her fingers. Her mouth began to stretch open, her

139

jaw snapping open, and her teeth became larger
and sharper, her nose flattened . . .

Wallace stood, startled, mouth open to make
a perfect 'O' and Amigo began to yelp. The
kitten still shook, burrowing its tiny head in its
paws. Mrs Tulip Sandtails was changing. She
was turning into a . . . tiger. The biggest cat of
them all.

'I thought you were allergic to cats!'
Wallace managed to dribble
out of his throat.
This made Mrs Tulip Sandtails
laugh in a deep croaky crackle. Her eyes
flickered and her paws padded about and her
nose sniffed her torn-up nightwear.

Amigo began to run in circles.

'What is happening? What are you?' Wallace managed to tumble out of his breathless chest.

'I'll tell you what is happening, you silly stupid boy,' sneered the talking tiger. 'The reason I can't own cats is because they are my favourite thing to EAT! The proof was in the name all along — you were just too naive to see it . . . CHEW LIPS AND TAILS!' She roared so loud the windows smashed and the china plates splintered to shards.

And then Mrs Tulip Sandtails, the tiger, stood on her now muscular hind legs and went to gobble up the tiny kitten in one gulp. But Amigo, being the brave and loyal dog that he was, leaped up in front of the tiny kitten, and in one fantastic bite bit the tiger's leg off, leaving a leg-short Mrs Tulip Sandtails weeping for mercy on the floor.

Nowadays, everything is very different at no. 64, where the white picket fence protects the beautiful blooming garden to a very stunning house. A large fat grey cat with apple green eyes lolls about in the morning sun, she is happy. On the doorstep sits a very brave and handsome dog, with an old bootlace around his neck. He is chewing the best cut of steak by the feet of his very best friend, a young gentleman.

'This is the life, eh, Amigo?' Wallace relaxes into the sun-warmed chair. 'Where's the maid with our snacks?'

Mrs Sandtails suddenly limps out of the house onto the front porch, carrying a tray piled high with bread and honey and warmed-up milk.

'Apologies for that little spill, sir, it's my wooden leg, it makes serving warm milk very tricky.'

'I know, Mrs Sandtails,' Wallace replied smiling. 'I know.'

'Darcy!' Poppy shouted up, and my pen jogged. 'The world is ended!' she cried up, and I knewed it was time to go downstairs.

Poppy was crying. She still hadn't eaten. She was

starving hungry and her cat was getting taken away.
And what if this Giorgio man was just simply a horrid
terror. Poor Pork. Poor Poppy. Poor everything that
begins with the letter 'P'.

'I hate you,' Poppy said to Dad as we waited in
the living room for Giorgio to arrive. Which even I
thought was a little harsh given that our own mum's
mum had died but Poppy just didn't seem to care.

'Don't say that,' Mum said, picking clumps of mud
off her gloves.

'I can say what I like if I mean it,' Poppy snapped,
stroking Pork's now tear-stained head. Pork was farting
in unison with Lamb-Beth, completely oblivious that
his true owner was coming to collect him any minute.

'You don't mean it.'

'I DO!'

Dad rolled his eyes and sipped his coffee, pretending
not to be fussed, but under his manly dad breath I
heard him say, 'I don't need this today.' And then he
wiped his face nearly right off into the palm of his
hand.

I felt sorry for him.

And Poppy.

And Pork.

'If you want to hate anybody, Poppy, hate me. I took Giorgio's number, I called him in the first place,' Mum argued.

'Yes, but you didn't get through, did you? Dad rang him back!'

'YOU hung up the phone on him, missy! How naughty is that?'

'Not very. It doesn't matter,' Poppy screamed, her eyes all red and sore and her cheeks purple with anger. 'Not when you are in *love*.' She wailed some more and clung to Pork, who didn't care and didn't budge.

'Ugh. You're in love with a cat,' Hector laughed.

'No, I am not, you stupid idiot ugly brat child. What do you know about anything except poo and farts and bogeys and snakes and zombies and wetting yourself and eating out-of-date Easter eggs?' *Whoa*, she really was being a ghastly piece of work now, as Hector only ate an out-of-date Easter egg once, *wow*, talk about *harbouring*. She continued, 'And even IFFED, and I mean IFFED, I even . . . I EVEN . . .

I EVEN am in love with Pork? It doesn't matter now, does it? Becaused *DAD* arranged for him to be taked away?'

'It's not Dad's fault,' I snapped. 'Silly Marnie Pincher was the one that gave him to us. She thought he was a stray.'

'It's nobody's fault. It's one of those things.' Mum rubbed her eyes now. This was getting silly. She had had enough.

'But there's a boy at my school who said their next-door neighbour just even stole their cat without even asking. They just kept on leaving out bowls of tinned tuna for it and it just moved in their house instead . . . why can't we just keep him the same as they did?'

'It's bad to do that, Poppy. Even though other people do so, it doesn't mean we do.'

'Oh!' Poppy sniffled. 'Why didn't Marnie check first that he wasn't a loved thing before she let me love him?' she warbled, her chin wobbling up and down.

I did feel sad for her. A. Lot. Even with the heaps of snot pouring out of her nostrils. Even with the fact she was being a thousand times more sad that a cat was being taken away than her own granny dying. But Pork had to go back to his true life. I could see both sides of the situation. When Lamb-Beth went missing it was the worst days of my life. I know how it feels to have a pet lost and have a pet found.

'She only gave him to us to get rid of the mice, remember, Poppy?' Dad tried. 'We all love Pork. We all don't want him to go.'

'Even you?' Poppy's tears sank into Pork's fur.

'Of course even me. I've got used to the big thing hanging around.'

And that, for some reason, made Poppy leap up, Pork in arms, and wrap herself around Dad for a big warm hug. Dad hugged her back tightly and kissed her head. Meanwhile Pork just sat there. Being squished. Staring out into space. He could be in the middle of the ocean for all he knew, and he still only knew how to make that one face. That one unimpressed face that said, *'Really?'* The only one of us that didn't care that Pork was leaving was, well, Pork.

The doorbell rang.

'Oh no!' Poppy began to cry, and then quickly hid

behind the sofa, tucking Pork under her arm, wanting to be so invisible, hoping that perhaps Giorgio would change his mind, or forget.

Giorgio wasn't a cat stealer at all. Or a tiger. Or evil. Or allergic. Obviously. He was tall and round. With white hair that sat like a puff of smoke on his head. He was a bit like sunshine in human form, like Mr Ray Beam, with his big round belly and happy face and tanned skin and rose petal-coloured cheeks.

His eyes were a soft bunny-rabbit brown. He wore a bright pink shirt covered in palm trees and parrots – which to be fair, I was quite envious of. Big crispy grey curly chest hairs poked through his shirt and he had a gold chain tangled up amongst the hairs. When he spoke, a big deep authentic kind Italian accent poured out of his mouth, as sweet as maple syrup and it wound its way into my ear like honey.

'Sorry-a to-a disturb-a you. On-a your Sunday.' Almost everything he said was chased up with the letter A.

'No, not at all.' Mum smiled. I caught her eyeing up his excellent shirt too.

'I-a am-a so-a pleased you-a called.' He grinned broadly, like a proud-of-himself bear.

'No, not a problem, I am just so sorry we didn't see your advertisement sooner.' Mum dusted some Lamb-Beth fur off her top, obviously wanting to a bit remove all traces of ALL animals that we love in one go. 'We weren't trying to steal him or anything. A friend found him, in the rain, and we had mice, so we said we would take him, and we didn't expect to have him so long but when nobody rang up to claim him we . . .' Mum began rushing out the storyline like we were all in big trouble. It reminded me of myself at school, when I am very quickly trying to sneak out of something naughty I've done.

Giorgio started to laugh. Hard.

'Sorry . . . did I say something wrong?' Mum quizzed, scratching her chin. Dad stood up and became all manly, just in case Giorgio was a fruitcake and he needed to take him down like a wrestler.

'I-a don't-a mean-a to-a be-a rude, is-a just-a that-a this-a cat . . . he-a couldn't catch-a mouse if it-a had-a been-a glued to his-a paws! He's rubbish!'

And to that we all laughed, because it was true. In our whole time of having Pork he hadn't caught ONE mouse. NOT ONE.

'Well-a, where is-a he?' Giorgio asked. 'Can-a I see him?' Peering around, Giorgio obviously wanted one of those TV chat show reunions with his big fat grey lump of a cat.

But he was behind the sofa with Poppy.

Mum lurched over the sofa and Poppy's big watery eyes flashed up at her. I felt sick and sad. Mum smiled to Giorgio awkwardly.

'My daughter, Poppy. I'm afraid she has rather taken to the cat. They have become very close.'

'I see.' Giorgio nodded, and then he too also peeped

over the sofa. 'Ahh, there-a he is-a. My boy.' Giorgio smiled, his crinkly eyes suffocated under his enormous pleased cheeks. 'Good-a to-a see you-a, my friend.'

Poppy stood up from behind the sofa and gently, with some effort, scooped up Pork and passed him to Giorgio. Pork consistently looked unimpressed and unfazed by the entire handover. 'There you go, Giorgio.' She looked down at the carpet; the bow that she always wears around her head flopped to the side, defeated.

'You-a have-a truly looked after him. He looks-a very happy-a and-a healthy.'

'Yes, I did.' Poppy blushed and wrapped her hands around one another.

'You-a look very happy, don't-a you, Dusty?' Giorgio nudged Pork, who now sat in his arms. Dusty? *Dusty?*

'Dusty?' Poppy asked, almost disgusted, suddenly dropping her *feel sorry for me* act.

'Yes. That's his name.'

'Dusty? Is that because of his grey fur?' Poppy added.

'No. It's-a short-a for-a Dustbin because all this-a cat does-a is eat!' And then we all laughed again. 'He's a dustbin! What-a did-a you-a name him?' Giorgio stroked Pork, who gently closed his eyes in peace.

'Pork,' Poppy blurted.

'Well-a, that's-a perfect name for him. We can-a call-a him Dusty Pork.'

'SIR Dusty Pork,' Hector added.

Giorgio showed his teeth in joy – he had one of those excellent laughs that make you spill your head right back. 'Very good-a. Sir Dusty Pork. The oldest salami in the deli!'

Poppy tried not to look at Pork. Lamb-Beth cowered in the corner, wincing in sadness. We knew it was time to say goodbye to Pork and to Giorgio. They were a family and they *belonged*. No matter how much we loved Pork ourselves, he wasn't really ours to love. He was a borrowed love.

We saw Giorgio to the door. Poppy began to pack all of Pork's belongings up. His plastic milk bowl, his mouse toy with the bell inside, the scrap of wool that he liked to play with, his cat treats. She handed the bag

to Giorgio. 'Oh, and he likes to dress up in babygros and wear bonnets, he loves sleepovers and Chinese food and his favourite best colour is pink.' She smiled. 'Oh, and breaking the rules. He loves that.'

'Pink, eh?' Giorgio belly-laughed. 'Sounds-a like him.'

'Will you remember all of that?' Poppy seemed concerned, as if she was a new mum sending Pork off with a babysitter for the evening. 'Call me if you forget anything,' she added. This made Mum bite her lip in sad love.

Waving Giorgio out and taking turns to cuddle Pork, Lamb-Beth winding in figure-of-eights around our ankles, Giorgio suddenly turned to us and said, 'Hey, have-a you-a lovely people had your lunch?'

Chapter Eight

Giorgio didn't just live close. He basically lived walkie-talkie close. He lived close enough to *run to once you've flushed the chain and manage to reach before the flush runs out* close. And what was better: he owned an Italian restaurant. Yum. So much best food is from Italy.

It was a small café-like place. The tables were all wibbly wobbly with white tablecloths on them. Each table had a small salt and pepper, and a little vase with a tiny red flower inside. The restaurant was covered in black-and-white signed photographs of all different people that both Mum and Dad seemed to know the names of, but I didn't. They looked like actors and singers from the past. I could tell one was a boxer though, because he had those red gloves on. But obvs they weren't red. They were black and white because it was an old photograph, but I knew they were meant to be red. Unless of course maybe in the olden times everything was black and white? It must be because of the photographs. I would hate to live in black-and-white times . . . what would I wear? I'M SO GLAD they invented colour.

There are a few other people in there for lunch too and they all seem Italian themselves. THAT'S how you KNOW it must be a good Italian restaurant. They all stare at us when we sit down. People *always* seem to stare at our family.

Giorgio, with Sir Dusty Pork in his hands, showed us round. We saw the coffee machine, the ice cream (which looked delicious) in choco-late, pistachio, vanilla, coffee, lemon and strawberry flavours, and the fresh pasta and red sauce. He dropped Sir Dusty Pork to his feet, and he

155

instantly began tiptoeing about the place in complete comfortable familiarity, sniffing and winding around the tables and chairs. Amazing how cats never cherish anything – it already felt as though we never existed to him. *Whatever, Pork. Thanks for nothing. You'll end up a LONELY alley cat, my friend, one of these days* . . . Come to think of it . . . that IS how we ended up with him in the first place. Some of the waitresses and waiters got really happy when they saw Sir Dusty Pork and they lifted him up and snuggled him and smiled and the chef fed him ham. No wonder he was fat.

This really is a lovely home for a lovely cat.

'This-a is-a the real exciting bit.' Giorgio's eyes lit up as he showed us the biggest brick fireplace you have ever seen, and at the back a huge fire roared on top of charcoaled cindered logs, its yellow flames licking the blackened walls.

'What's that for?' Poppy asked, her cheeks already glowing from the warmth of the oven.

'Pizza!' Giorgio said grandly. 'You want?'

For the next hour we made dough, rolled it out, tossed it about exactly in the same way as those men

and women in the stripy T-shirts do at Pizza Express, like spinning floppy soft records on a record player of a finger. Then we each laid our dough out and decorated it however exactly we pleased with cheese and tomato, olives and ham, pepperoni, mushrooms, peppers, sweetcorn, onion. Poppy did hers in a smiley face. Which was a good sign that she had so much cheered up.

The pizzas went into the oven on these long hot shovels and came out moments later completely crisped up and the cheese all melty. Giorgio showed us how to

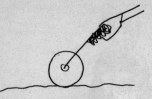

slice them up with a real-life professional pizza slicer and how to sprinkle on parmesan and how to even use those ginormous wooden pepper grinders too.

It was the most delicious thing I had ever eaten. The cheese was all stringy and toasty, the base was flat and crispy and the crust was chewy and it tasted so much better because I even made it.

Mum sipped on red wine and Dad scooped the ice cream out with Giorgio, piling the colours up into creamy sweet ice mountains. We were so happy. Even though Granny was dead.

'Come-a whenever you like.' Giorgio patted us on the shoulders as he sent us, bellies full, plod-plod-plodding home. Yes, cat-less, but perhaps friend-*plus*.

A happy story after all.

Chapter Nine

It's Friday. A flick in the face is not the bestest most nicest way to be woked up.

'Oi,' he says. 'Oi.'

There he is. In all his splendorous terrificness.

My Uncle Adrian.

In a bright turquoise wig.

'Wakey-wakey, lazybones!' he says in that voice I love so much.

'Uncle Adrian!' I leap out of the bed and throw my arms around him. He smells of aeroplane and moisturizer and aftershave. 'I didn't know you were coming!'

'I had to, obviously, with the news.'

'I'm so happy you're here!' I roar, and reach round him, hugging him close.

'Me too! And I'm glad you're happy to see me too! Just not with that morning breath, girlfriend!'

I laugh and put my hand over my mouth. Morning breath smells like an uncleaned goldfish bowl. Stale and stagnant. Uncle Adrian has always been a wind-up though, and he nuzzles me, even with the terrible breath. He then scoops me out of the bed, lifts me high above his head, twirls me round and round and throws me down onto the bed. He picks up one of my – unused, as I NEVER brush these locks – hairbrushes, and sings a high-pitched Madonna song into it and shakes his bum.

160

'Let's go and wake up Popsicle!' He grins naughtily. He turns round to let me clamber up onto his back. 'We're coming for you, Poppy!' he wails, not even caring WHO he wakes up. He lurks and snoops like a giant, grunting and snuffling, juddering me about on his back, his turquoise wig bobbing about:

'Dum. Dum. Dummidy. Dum.

Dum. Dum. Dummidy. Dum.

Poppy, Poppy, here we come!' he booms around the house.

Poppy is snoozing away in her bed, her arms up over her head like a flamenco dancer, elegant and perfect.

'Morning to the best Sixties bob in SOUTH LONDON! BIG UP!' he shouts and Poppy shudders, jumps up and then when her eyes properly open and de-blur and she sees Uncle Adrian, she squeals in happiness. She wraps her arms around him and he tickles her, 'Girl, you is *Sweatsville* up in those armpits!' Poppy giggles. He grins back, scooping her up to standing, then he claps his hands and encourages Poppy to strut along her mattress. 'Work it, work it, work it, work the catwalk . . . uh-huh, honey . . .' He parades Poppy up

161

and down her bed as though she is on a catwalk, and Poppy gets all the faces of the models SO good it's hilarious.

'Where's HECTORIOUS?' He shouts his name out as though he is a Greek god. 'Let's get him!'

Poppy and I both, now, are stuck to Adrian's back, all elbows and kneebows and arms and legs, flailing and swinging and trying our best not to let one part of our bodies touch the floor. We cling to Adrian's back as though he is a big ape and we are his baby monkeys.

Hector is snoring.

'Attention! Hector Burdock – wow . . . he is SO *big!* Can't believe it. Man! He makes me feel well old. Ahh, look at him sleep.' We all stand over Hector. He *is* quite sweet, I guess. Upturned nose, wonky teeth, big eyes, freckles, curly hair. 'Them girls and boys better WATCH *out* when this one grows up!'

Uncle Adrian claps his hands and Hector wakes, rubbing his eyes. He looks Uncle Adrian up and down, in his turquoise wig and giant bright blue eyes, and says, 'Who on earth is that?'

Mum and Dad are still asleep. Or pretending to be, I suppose. Uncle Adrian used to have a real key to ours. But then once he abused his position and invited a trillion and four friends over and had a 24-hour rave while we were on holiday. So that got confiscated and never replaced. Uncle Adrian doesn't mind. He doesn't like responsibility anyway. Dad must have let him in and sneaked off to bed for more dozing.

I can't believe I have survived the hideous ghastly week of school with the most annoying Clementine. ALL WEEK she has been weasling her way up my nostrils rehearsing her stupid song, 'warming her voice' up and gargling salt water to 'protect' her tonsils. The only thing she needs to protect is her stupid noodle-like hair from getting covered in too much soy sauce.

That wasn't even a good joke.

I'm so glad no one is reading this.

I honestly don't think her song is even going to be a shock for anybody, as we've all heard her do it so many times. And when she does the high bits her nostrils flare and her eyes all close and pinch shut and tremble and she does these annoying movements with her hands like she is a blind person trying to swat a fly.

AND I AM SO LIVID WITH WILL, like I can't even say, but I have to say so I am. I was really hoping he was going to be my wingman/boy the entire night and run away with me and build a den and stuff our faces and perhaps even coax my dad into somehow picking us up early and running back to my house and instead just having our own adventure there.

But NO. One second of my back being turned and not only is he up for going to the sleepover, but now he is LOOKING FORWARD to it. Him and his stupid boy mates – yes, again I know it's a nice thing to do – have decided to try and raise a bit more for charity by seeing how many kick-ups they can do for the entire sleepover. BORING. DRY. CRUSTY. ANNOYING. Which means I will have nobody to even hang out with. FUMING. And I will NOT be forced to be one of those stupid senseless females that linger around boys while they do stuff like kick a ball.

Grrrrr.

And now, because Will is so excited for the

sleepover, he won't even hear a bad word against the whole entire thing so I have to trap every thought about my reluctance about the event and hatred towards Clementine to myself.

That's why I'm so glad Adrian is here. I can't WAIT to talk trash with him and get all this bundle of burden off my chest. You shouldn't really anyway do gossiping at school with friends. Really and truly, you can only do real actual gossiping with your family because they can be trusted one thousand per cent. I like to think it's because they are the best at keeping secrets but I think it's actually because they just don't care. Or really listen. But it makes you feel much better.

We sit around for tea, with a breakfast of amazing American candy: Jellybeans and Nerds and Jolly Ranchers. You know when something is *not* meant for your insides when it is the same colour as Hector's toys. America makes the best sweets but not chocolate. It's NOT as good as England's by any stretch – it's very Easter-Eggy, *cheap* Easter-Eggy – but as far as breakfasting goes, it beats cornflakes and Rice Krispies.

Uncle Adrian calls us his 'lunatics' or 'hooligans' . . . and sometimes if he's feeling mushy, he calls us 'the reason' he 'lives'.

I can't wait to make Uncle Adrian a cup of tea to show him that I am now mostly extremely capable of this exact job and no longer have playdough hands of babyness. That I can actually *apply* myself. But I don't want to make a big deal out of the matter. If I get too excited about making him tea he will doubt my adult authenticity; no true growed-up mature person of wisdom gets excited to make tea for someone else. I lean against the counter, all casual, like how Mum does.

'Tea, Adrian?' I try and say, all normal.

'Tea? I'll make it, Darcy,' he says.

'Don't be silly . . . it's no bother.' I get to it, just like how Mum would, as though it's not even a thing. Poppy rolls her eyes right round. Jealousy will lead her to nowhere but a sad and lonely life.

'Can you make tea now then? Big girl!'

'I nearly canned too!' Poppy yells.

'She can't,' I mutter.

'Nearly.'

'Well, I'd love a cup of tea, thank you, Darcy. The tea on the aeroplane is horrible. They give it to you only half full and in an ugly plastic cup.'

'How do you take it?' *Oh, SORRY about me and my tea language!*

'Strong, milky and a sugar and a half.' He smiles. Trust Uncle Adrian to have pudding tea like that. The kettle starts to rumble.

'You don't still have that weird tiny *dog*-sheep thing, do you?' Adrian asks, looking about.

'We've never had a sheepdog, if that's what you mean?' Poppy says back. She whistles for Lamb-Beth, who within moments enters dozily.

'NO! You've got the reverse – a dog-sheep, honey. That weirdo little fluffy sprat thing. I would LOVE to get my scissors and shear up that little barnet!'

Uncle Adrian is a hairdresser for his job. Which is

perfect for him. He is always only joking though, and he collects up Lamb-Beth and brings her to his knees. She licks his hands immediately.

'Lamb-BREATH!' Uncle Adrian shrieks at Lamb-Beth's breath. 'What you been eating, Bunny-on-Legs? Garlic croutons and mackerel pâté?'

'No!' Hector snaps back, trying to defend Lamb-Beth. 'She eats her armpits.' Lamb-Beth does a nice juicy fart at this moment.

Uncle Adrian awkwardly drops Lamb-Beth back down on the floor. 'You hooligans sicken me . . . and I love it! Right . . . let's see what magic I have in my case.'

Uncle Adrian takes us through to the living room, then he sets his case down and we all sit about it. It is a battered bright orange case that looks well-travelled and exciting. He unzips the seal and peels open the lid.

Inside looks like the contents of a fancy dressing-up box: curly wigs, blond wigs, Afro wigs, clown wigs. Tubs of glitter in every colour, a feather boa, a fur coat, high heels(?!), an old-fashioned telephone(?!), sunglasses, a hairdryer . . .

'Where's your actual stuff, Uncle Adrian?' Poppy looks concerned.

'This *is* my actual stuff.' He begins rummaging through. 'Wait until you see my bling!' Uncle Adrian opens up a navy silk pouch and scatters heaps of what looks like pirate treasure onto the floor – gold chains, silver necklaces and jewels, except it's all plastic and weighs as light as a sponge.

'Why did you bring all this fancy dressing-up stuff?' Hector doesn't understand.

'Why not?' He shrugs. 'Real clothes are so boring.'

He is right. I can't believe I sacrificed my true colourful identity for fear of being laughed at by stupid bug-eyed Clementine. I had let my whole entire family name down. I really did need a boost of my true-to-himself uncle.

'Let's dress up and take pictures!' Poppy squeals.

'Great idea!' Uncle Adrian screeches and begins to dress us up.

'Oh, wait! We can't!' Poppy shakes her head. 'We've got school today.'

'Does it look like you're going to school?'

'But it's a Friday, and Mum will be angry at us!' Poppy whispers.

'Don't worry yourself, cupcake, Uncle Adrian has sorted it.' And he gives us a wink. I think this was an *organized* surprised visit.

We spend the rest of the morning in fancy dress. Poppy keeps wanting to get Mum and Dad to come down and see us having fun, she wants them to be dressed up like us, but Uncle Adrian tells us to let them rest. I think this perhaps was a bit to give Mum and Dad a break, so I distract Poppy by pretending to be a rapper in the fake bling and the fur coat. She is cracking up. Hector does not hesitate whatsoever to be a fully dressed-up girl – he loves the high heels, especially crick-cracking around in them on the kitchen tiles for the most effective sound effect. We have so much fun, showing off and prancing about. Forgetting ourselves a bit for a short while, which is allowed, you know.

Eventually Mum and Dad come down looking well rested and much happier than yesterday. When Mum sees Uncle Adrian she flings her arms around him and they touch head on head. Like penguins do. It is like their foreheads are magnets to each other, their hands are all holding, they are connected. They are probably remembering so much about what makes them bound: their school photos, their scabby knees, their arguments, their pet family dog, their trips to the cinema, when they met a baby monkey at the fair, when they built a den by the river, when Uncle Adrian wedgied that boy in front of everyone because he said Mum's freckles were 'ugly', when Mum went mental on holiday in Spain because a boy called Robert pushed Adrian in the deep end of the pool when he was just a toddler and he nearly drowned . . . and now they are all growed up. Different but the same. And the way, although from different homes, they were brought together, under Granny's roof, who raised these two unlikely strangers as brother and sister and now as best friends. Not a drop of blood the same, but their hearts beating to the same rhythm.

I look at Poppy and Hector. The closest connect time we have is wiping our bogeys on each other's backs when the other one isn't looking.

'Come on, Darcy, you've got the sleepover at school to get ready for, haven't you?' Mum says over hot cross buns. I was really hoping that she had forgotten. THAT'S obviously why the other two gotted the day off. To have heaps of fun with Uncle Adrian while I was sent to the horror chambers of school.

'A sleepover? At school?' Uncle Adrian cackles. 'How bleak is that?'

'I know, right?' I lick my finger and scoop up the remaining cinnamon crumbs.

'Such a shame. I was going to take us all to the BBQ place down the road and get us something fatty and disgusting to eat.'

'YAY!' Poppy and Hector shriek in unison.

This annoys me. 'Can't you wait until tomorrow to eat fatty and disgusting things?'

'It's half price on Fridays and the belly don't wait,' Uncle Adrian tries to explain. 'Not for no one.'

I feel like throwing a right temper storm, but I equally want to look matured like a fragrant old cheese. But I am SO jealous. I don't want to go to this ghastly sleepover. I really don't.

I know Mum wants me to go so it's one less child to worry about what to *do* with, but also she thinks it's good to put oneself through things you don't necessarily *want* to do. 'You never know . . .' she says. 'You might meet a new friend.'

I don't WANT a new friend. I want to play with Uncle Adrian. He's my main friend. I want to sit here and chill and play all day and eat BBQ food, and *Bob's your uncle* the sleepover happens without me being there. Except Bob is not my uncle. My uncle is

173

Adrian, who has come at the WRONG TIME OF MY LIFE.

I pull a card out of the opportunity hat in my head. 'I think it's more valuable and precious if I spend time with Uncle Adrian. We should spend some quality time together, don't you think?' I try, and flutter my eyelashes.

'Don't pull that one, sweetie! Ain't *nobody* falling for that!' Uncle Adrian cracks up with laughter, unconvinced, and then everybody begins to laugh. Hector. Poppy. Mum. Uncle Adrian. Even probably Lamb-Beth. All at me. Laughing. But not Dad. He KNOWS not to be in MY bad books. He just sits, rubbing his temples.

The laughter makes me grow madder and madderer. So madderer like an Angrosaurus-rex because I am so hateful of this sleepover and so angry they are going to have fun without ME! I am mad like a thick ghastly sewage is about to inhabit my entire flesh and bones and do something so vile and dangerous and I just open my mouth and scream something NASTY, something that will REALLY ruin their fun and plummet them on a fast way trip to Guilt Land . . .

'You are the most disgusting heartlessless family in the entire world of families! Are you all completely blind to the fact that our GRANNY has died? That's right. She is DEAD. And all you lot want to do is eat chicken wings and ribs and other delicious things, like probably corn. On a cob. And beans. And chips. And slurp Coca-Cola, gossiping about how happy and ALIVE you all are! Meanwhile I will be LEFT OUT. At a wretched school sleepover. Not eating BBQ food. Probably just considering how Granny is dead. But don't worry. I'll just do it on behalf of everyone, seeing as though you are too caught up in having an absolutely fantastic time to care! We should all be together at a time like this. But, oh no, you all seem *quite* content to farm me off.'

Nobody says a word. Blink. Blink. Look down. Silence.

'Too far,' Dad says. 'You've gone too far this time, Darcy. Get your pyjamas on and get in the car.' He is NOT happy. 'NOW!' his voice booms, and it's as if every window cracks, it's as if all the pictures fall off the walls.

'But we're early . . .' I try. Tears bubble and brew up in my eyes. They shake. My dad is a monster right now.

'I MEAN IT!' Dad roars, and the way he shouts at me makes me jump and makes Hector burst into tears.

Poppy awkwardly hums and dances out of the room, pretending like she has somewhere to be.

Adrian looks into his mug.

Mum puts her head in her hands.

I am the worst.

I am the monster.

I pound up the stairs. I want to cry an ocean.

I am just totally livid that Hector and Poppy are getting to hang with Adrian for the entire time. And have BBQ. I am also gutted because there is no way on this earth, now that Granny has croaked it, that I can happily put on bright colourful pyjamas. Because she made the horrid curtain-jamas for me, so I am obliged. It was the last and nicest thing she ever did for me. I feel weird putting on my recycled curtains, as Granny made them for me and I don't want to make Mum upsetted or weird, but I also don't want to have all her dead skin bits on me. Dust is actually blitzed-up skin and hair and so there is bound to be some of it on my PJs. I don't care how dead you are. Still gross. Fuming. Typically. And now not only am I attending the sleepover I will most probably be EARLY too, like an eager beaver.

I don't even have time to say goodbye to my loved ones as Dad is on a furious mission to ship me off to this sleepover as quickly as possible because I am so hated.

Dad drives me to the sleepover. I had wanted to come with Will in the car so I didn't feel all exposed like a big red spot on a pale person's forehead, but it didn't seem appropriate to go around making plans when I was clearly the most hated person in my family. Besides, Will was coming with all his annoying foot-ball friends.

Then I remember. I am going to be a loner the entire evening. NO! And to top it ALL off, Clementine is SINGING. TONIGHT. YUCK. YUCK. YUCK. I can't be bothered for everyone to just be loving her up so much and hanging on her every single word and watch her stupid pop-star impersonation dancing and the ugly faces she pulls as if she's having a giant poo.

NO.

Dad doesn't say a single word to me on the way there. I beat myself up for being such a wretched nasty selfish ghastly brat brute child that was even evil enough to hope to use my granny's death as some guilt scheme to be able to avoid going to the sleepover, but then again I am only a human bean with many shades to my personality, exactly like a rainbow just with skin wrapped around me. It looks like there is no avoiding it; the sleepover is happening. I am doomed. To endure all this wretched nasty hell.

I am really having to go. Aren't I? 360-degree eyeball roll to THAT one. Why did we have to have money problems at this time of our lives? Why oh why can't I be going in gorgeous glamorous all growed up pyjamas? Not CURTAINS. I sniff a bit, and then I sneak a look at Dad and feel even more guilty brat child from pond of scum and slime and cat poo who Doesn't Care about her family. Dad has PROBLEMS. Dad doesn't even have a job and here I am moaning about having to go to some lameo wameo jameo sleepover that's meant to be fun.

'Dad?' I try. I want to show him I can be a big growed-up helpful Darcy.

He grunts back.

'You know if you need us to, you know, get jobs to make money, we can.'

He snaps at me, 'Not you too! You sound just like your mum! We don't NEED money. We are FINE for money. Can't everybody just get off my back? I will sort this. OK? Just stop it!'

Tears whirlpool up in my eyes. All drippy. I am sad. I was only making a suggestion. I can't even do that properly. Very quickly Dad notices that he snapped a bit too much.

'I'm sorry. I should not have shouted at you. You don't need to get a job, Darcy. You can't anyway, because you need to write as much as possible so that I can retire and live off your royalties and you can buy me a lovely big castle with a swimming pool and a car and I'll eat the poshest ham that money can buy.'

A warm feeling explodes in me that makes me so happy.

'Actually, writers are actually quite poor, Dad,' I say glumly.

'Well, in that case you better get to work quick, quit school and become a lawyer,' he jokes.

'But I do wish I could help. I just wish I was a millionaire that needed some wood to be built into something because I would employ you nonstop.'

'I know you would, baby girl.' He winks at me and it's summer in my heart.

I hope he doesn't really want me to be a lawyer. I would hate to wear that grey wig.

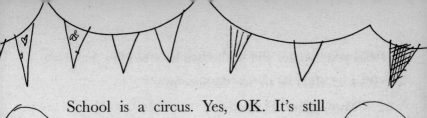

School is a circus. Yes, OK. It's still concrete and grey and boring and hideously ugly, but it's covered in balloons and bunting to try and make it look more better and actually I am a bit impressed and get a little beetle of excitement born in my tummy that grows wings and begins to dart about. Oh, my goshness, that's disgusting, it makes me sound like some Mother of Bugs and Creepy Crawlies. Yuck. I take that back . . .

Big speakers blare tinny pop music out onto the London streets, making passers-by double take. There are parents and family members taking photographs of everybody dressed in their jimjams. Some have gone to town with their outfits and are sporting dressing gowns and slippers; they've even brought their teddy bears. But only the olderer ones, because they think it's *ironic*. None of us youngers would ever DREAM of bringing our teddies into school. Like I

181

told you, we are still in the 'we hate teddies' lie phase. It's a HARD lie to live. Believe me.

'You ready?' Dad asks.

'As I'll ever be,' I grunt, and then feel a bit proud of myself because that's one of those sentences that people say in films when they are cool. We kiss awkwardly on the cheek and I wave goodbye.

The moment he drives away I realize in the stress of it all I forgot to ask him for money. It's a charity sleepover and I don't have a single penny to give towards charity. If I had asked anyway, Mum would only be cross at me that I mentioned the M word anyway. (M being money obviously, not Mum, she doesn't hate me THAT much.) I think perhaps this will act as another excuse to not go but thinking about it, I think I've rinsed all my excuses for today. I just have to suck it up. Like a hoover.

Walk. Walk. Walk.

I make my way to the school entrance and stupid annoying Clementine and her vile gaggle of idiots have basically taken over the entire charity sleepover like it's their actual birthday party. If there is one thing more worserer and irritating than Clementine it's *trying to be nice and charitable* Clementine with her fake puppy-dog eyes and over-shiny bubblegumglossed lips and curly Super-Noodled ridiculous hair springing everywhere like octopus tentacles on a sugar high. If you ask me, her attire was *not* what I would call pyjamas by any stretch of the word. If I slept in *that* outfit I would wake up with bruises on me . . . they are THAT tight. A little stupid pink vest top with red hearts dotted all over it and a tiny pair of glittery gold hot pants that her bum cheeks were gobbling up. Gross.

My hand trembles. I have no money. Not a thing to put inside the bucket. What am I going to do? All I can hear is the clunks of everybody else's coins as they land in the bucket. My coin will fall like air. Because there is no coin to fall.

'So good to see you, thanks for coming.' She greets everybody as if school is HER house. She speaks in a tacky sarcastic voice as we all walk in in our stupid outfits. She delegated the job of holding the bucket of money for the charity to a member of her *staff*, who stands in awkward awe under the willowy trunk of Clementine.

'Welcome, thanks so much, you look *amazing* . . .' she charms through gritted toothed forced smiles. 'You look so hot, what a *mega* babe . . .' she lies to a girl in front who clearly took the idea of *wear what you wear to bed* too literally and is wearing a snot-covered track-suit, her hair a giant spray of knot and ginger tangle.

I am next in line, and I overhear Clementine's bossy snarl to her *assistant* to 'shake the bucket more'. She licks her teeth as though there is lipstick on them, and then says, 'It makes people give more money.' The assistant quickly begins to furiously shake the bucket and the twinkly bell of coins rings through the air.

'Darcy!' she sirens – she can't be nasty today, *this* is for charity. Best behaviour day, girlfriend, I think to myself. 'You look . . .' She is running her eyes up and down me. I thought her job was to collect money at the door, *not* to comment on our pyjamas. She tweaks

184

her tone, recovering from her high-pitched squeal and settles for, 'Mature.' She wraps her hands around each other. 'Money in the bucket, thank you, do have a *nice* time,' she continues, over-exaggerating her American accent by the power of 100.

'I forgot mine,' I murmur.

'You FORGOT?' she booms out in her big clucky voice, WANTING everybody to hear.

'Yes.' I bleach white. I feel sick. I sheepishly pretend to look in my pockets, as if I may have misplaced the money.

'Darcy Burdock, the sleepover is not *just* a REALLY good excuse to have fun and wear skimpy outfits and kiss boys. This is actually in aid of charity.'

I look puzzled. 'I wasn't . . .'

She continues, 'I mean, it's really irresponsible of you. I know times are hard for everybody but it's nice to think of others for a change.'

Another horrid girl nods in approval.

'I'm sorry,' I say. I just want to turn round and not go in. I can't BEAR apologizing to just a toad.

'Why did you forget?'

I am sick of this dissecting from her. *I forgot.* OK. But really? Do I need to be interrogated THIS much. The queue behind me is getting bigger and bigger, and people are listening.

I bite my lip. 'My granny died. I forgot because my granny died,' I bark.

'Oh.' Clementine lets out a burst of laughter. It's a shock type of laughter that I don't think she meant. She covers her mouth. 'That's fine, girls, let her through,' she says to the other bouncer girls and I walk right in.

I did it again. I really am rinsing this excuse. I am a terrible, terrible, ugly-on-the-inside girl.

I scurry inside. Mavis, the receptionist, waves at me from her little booth; she has a fluffy dressing gown on and then holds her mug up towards me, *cheersing* me. I go over to say *hi*. It's nice to see a familiar face. Mavis pulls the little glass shutter open.

'Hello, wee hen.'

'Hi, Mavis.'

'I don't suppose you're reading tonight, are you?'

'NO WAY!' I laugh. 'Not me.'

'I didn't think you would, but you never know. You might have treated me.'

'Sorry, Mavis. It's not my thing, you know . . . reading out loud and everything.'

'I understand. I'm chained to my desk all night anyway, so it's probably for the best!' She sips her tea. 'What gorgeous PJs, where are they from?'

'They are old curtains.'

'Old curtains! But they are beautiful. Let me see?' Mavis felt the fabric in between her finger and thumb. 'Beautiful, just beautiful. Who made these then? Mum?'

'My granny, mainly.'

'I'd like a pair! Tell her to make me a pair!'

'I can't. She's dead.'

Mavis was NOT expecting THAT response. I'm just telling anyone that will listen now! 'Oh, wee girl, I'm sorry to hear that.' She held my hand in her warm palm, and I had to remind myself that *wee* in Scottish means *little* and NOT urine.

'No, it's OK. She wasn't my best grandma.'

Mavis couldn't help turn a smile up at that, even

though it's inappropriate. 'Let me know if you want anybody to talk to. I do love it when you come and sit in here with me.'

'I won't, but I will.'

'You *won't* but you *will*?'

I laugh. 'I mean, I won't need to talk to you about that, but I will come and talk to you about something soon . . . not *something*, just about . . . you know . . . anything.'

'And you must bring a story. I would love to have one of your stories soon.'

'Yes, I will.'

'Now off you go, go have fun, hen.'

Fun? Watching Clementine sing? Trying to follow Will around with his annoying football mates kicking a ball up and down one thousand times?

I follow the sound of excited shrieks through to the main hall. Puddles of people cluster together in little groups, *all* in their pyjamas, laughing and joking, commenting on their outfits. There is a popcorn machine pelleting puffed-up corn out and the smell is all homely and cinema-like. A man with a curly moustache and stripy suit whisks flamingo-pink clouds of candyfloss and a woman turns fat hot dogs on a grill. The smell is sweet and thick. I can't see Will anywhere and to pretend to look as though you are not looking for anybody is really hard. I go to get a drink and look busy.

'Burdockington!' Olly Supperidge yells from across the hall. You have *got* to be joking. He wears a

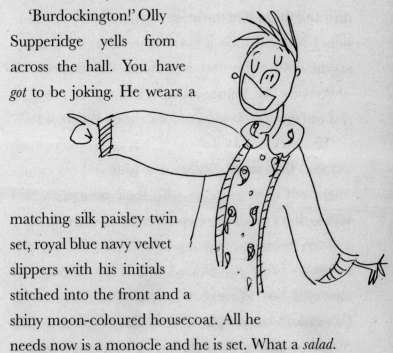

matching silk paisley twin set, royal blue navy velvet slippers with his initials stitched into the front and a shiny moon-coloured housecoat. All he needs now is a monocle and he is set. What a *salad*.

'Is that what you wear to bed?' I splutter over my polystyrene cup of lukewarm hot chocolate.

'Errrrrr. No. If I wore what I *actually* wear to bed I would get arrested,' he snubs. 'Gotta love a birthday suit.'

Do you? Oh, *yuck*. Olly Supperidge goes to bed naked and he has just told me. I shake the image out of my head, collect it into a big iron box, padlock it shut and throw it in the brain river inside my imagination. I NEVER want it to resurface. Ever.

'So I wore the next best thing.' He inspects his fingernails. 'My lounge attire.'

I roll my eyes. *Whatever.* I look about. Where is Will?

'I haven't seen Will about if that's who you're looking for,' Olly sniffs. 'Rumour is him and his chums might not even grace us with their presence . . . I mean, that's pretty poor considering it's for charity.'

I am feeling quite guilty myself. I am the one that forgot to bring my money! Still. I do LOADS for charity. I buy so much of my clothes from charity shops. And books. But it's that smug look that Olly Supperidge wears so well that's grinding my gears. I squint at him; my eyes begin dicing him up like sushi.

'My, my, if looks could kill.' He pops a boiled sweet

into his mouth and it audibly clatters on his teeth. I can tell it's sour because he pulls his cheeks in. The sweet is already making his tongue go blue which is giving me an enormous surge of pleasure.

'He's coming. He wouldn't miss this,' I snap.

'Yes, but there's an entry fee, Darcy, even if it *is* for charity, and we *all* know that Will's big sister hardly has money to spare . . . I mean . . .'

'You mean *what*? What do you mean?' My blood begins to boil. NOT another fight. We still haven't recovered from the food fight we had before that left me suspended and gave me a nosebleed from a flailing jacket potato. Already, just one second into the charity sleepover, and I'm ready to attempt to singe his face with lukewarm hot chocolate. Well, try to, at least.

'Watch it, Burdock, get a sense of humour . . .' He shakes his head and puts his hands up as if I'm about to arrest him. I bite my tongue. 'But don't get Will to pay for it. I'll get it for your next birthday.' He patters off.

Stay calm, Darcy. Stay calm, Darcy. I can't. I charge after him, ready to dollop my entire body weight onto his back and rip his absurd little twin set to shreds.

AHHHHHHHHHHHHHHHH! I'M COOOOOOO-MMMMIING FOR YOU . . . WATCH OUT!

'Darcy!' It's Maggie. Right in my face. She has on a really amazing rainbow nightie that I am quite obviously jealous about.

'Hi, Maggie,' I hiss, my eyes still drilling the back of Olly's head.

'What's wrong?' Maggie looks around to my eye line. *OH, HIM.* 'He's so disgusting. He's been going around telling everybody that he sleeps in the nude! I had to blank *that* image out. Could you imagine?' Maggie then does an impression of Olly getting ready for bed and trying to look all handsome in the mirror, and it's really funny and I can't help it. I spill into laughter. 'Hey, I've got to go, we're doing an interpretive dance about endangered species and we have to rehearse quickly before.'

'Oh, cool, OK.' I smile, feeling my heart rate gently simmer down. 'What animal do you play?'

'A turtle. I wanted to be a chimpanzee but they

gave it to someone else, but that's only because she has a monkey costume. Anyway. Does she have a tie-dye nightie? *Oh no*, she does not.' I laugh, and Maggie laughs too and walks away smiling.

'Look forward to your dance,' I shout after her.

'Don't!' she calls back. 'It's terrible.'

I try to keep hold of the new smile Maggie gave me painted on my face but I feel like a sad clown. Inside I am not happy. I shouldn't even be here. Granny's died and we have not very much money and Pork has gone and Poppy's upsetted and Will said he would be here. Even if he was just going to spend the entire evening kicking a ball up and down, at least I'd still feel his presence, but in actual fact he is completely nowhere to be seen and now I can't leave because I don't want Mavis at Reception to feel sorry for me, or Clementine or Olly to see that I am feeling so rejected and do all that whisper business about me. And then to top it off my family hate me probs and are all just eating BBQ food without me and having LOLs.

A song wails out of the big speakers and everybody jumps up and screams and shouts to it and starts

dancing, sipping hot chocolate and eating candyfloss. But I don't like this song. I like The Beatles and Eminem. And I don't like ANYONE here, at all. Mrs Ixy, the first teacher I ever metted at big school, spots me and clip-clops over. She is wearing a bright red onesie. And high heels.

'I know . . . I know . . .' she says, 'but I don't own slippers – they make my feet too hot.'

'I wasn't going to say that.' I smile. It's actually quite nice to see her.

'So . . . you're not reading anything tonight? I didn't see your name in the performances.'

'No. It's not for me.'

'I don't blame you,' Mrs Ixy says out of the corner of her mouth. 'Even just wearing this stupid thing makes me feel ridiculous.'

'You look nice,' I say.

'So do you, those are nice pyjamas. I had you down for something a little . . . *louder*.'

I blush. 'I'm just going to use the toilet,' I say.

'Sure, the girls' that way are really full. I think Clementine and entourage have sort of "taken over" it as some kind of "dressing room", if you get my drift. Honestly, it smells like Disneyland in there. Just pink and *bleugh*. So feel free to use the ones right by the gym cupboard. I trust you won't go in there and throw all the cricket bats about.' She laughs.

'Thanks, Mrs Ixy.'

'Come back and keep me company once you're done. This is my post for the night. You can get me a hot chocolate.'

I frown. I don't even have money to put in the charity bucket, let alone buy my teacher a hot chocolate.

'Don't worry, they are free!' she jokes, then immediately turns her smile into a growl as she has to discipline a boy in the year above who got too overexcited and flykicked another boy in the head.

I didn't really need the toilet. I wonder if she knew that?

Into the corridor, where the music sound is dull, like a set of headphones underwater. I creep around, sticking my body to the walls, feeling like a thief in the night. Except there is nothing in this school that anybody in their right minds would want to steal. The gym cupboard door is open and so I charge in there to get some peace time. The light is off, but because the door is open a stream of gold light shines an arrow of brightness into the room.

In here is all the gym stuff that I am not used to because I'm really not a gym kind of person. Bats and rackets, cricket sets, basketballs, netballs, footballs, hockey sticks and then all the lost property stuff too. Uniforms and trainers and bags and jumpers. And then piles and piles and piles of mats all stacked on top of each other like a loaf of sliced bread. The whole room smells of dried mud and sweaty cheesy feet and plastic.

I climb up the mats, feeling exactly like how the princess from that story *The Princess and the Pea* must have felt when she climbs up her big huge tower of a bed. It's harder than I thought, but reasonably fun. I do wish Will was here because he would love this. When I get to the top I throw myself dramatically onto my back, and breathe out loud in the darkness.

And then I hear a . . . *pssst*.

Chapter Ten

I scream and jump up.

'Hello?' I whisper out into the darkness. It's coming from the end of the mats, where the light doesn't reach to, and because the mats are piled so high up it's very close to the ceiling. Is it a *ghost*? A talking rat? A monster that has been created from all the lost property – from odd trainers and smelly socks and ratty jumpers – and mud, and has been banished to live in the gym cupboard? 'He-l-lo?' I croak again, and my own voice terrifies me.

My heart begins to beat quickly and I start to scamper back down the mats as quick as I can. *Great.*

My ONE exploring session on my own HAD to go wrong, didn't it? And just as I get halfway down, a hand reaches down and it feels like I've been scooped up to the mats again single-handedly. I am too afraid even to scream, even when the hand lets go.

A torch, under my face, lights up.

'Who are you?' the voice snaps. It's a girl's voice, I think, but I can't be sure. It's not mean but it's bossy and confident and young, and I don't recognize it.

'Who am *I*?' I bite back. 'Who are *you*?'

'I asked first.' Yes, she's definitely a girl. About my age too.

'You didn't exactly give me a chance, did you?' I am arguing in the darkness with what could easily be a Lost Property Monster as the light of the torch continues to flash in my face.

'Why are you here?'

'I could ask you the same question.' Had to give it the attitude, didn't I? LEARN to button it, Darcy B!

'Give me your hand again.'

'No.'

'*GIVE* me your hand.'

'You nearly just dislocated it when you dragged me up here!'

'Give it to me. And don't be so pathetic.' She reaches for my hand in the darkness and I snatch it back.

'Why should I trust you?' I frown.

'You shouldn't,' she replies quickly, and her voice warms, 'but I won't hurt you.'

Given that this creature seems to have night vision, strength and the power of, basically, a superhero, I have to oblige. I lay my hand inside hers.

'Unless I *have* to,' she adds, and then she clamps my hand, *hard*, like a vice to show me her strength, not that I needed reminding.

I feel almost paralysed, I can't move. She begins to

prod and probe my hands. Her fingers are soft and smooth from what I can tell. Who *is* this wizard child? Where is Will? *Surely soon he will come looking for me?* She begins to mutter under her breath. I can't hear much because my heart is thudding through my chest so loudly and I'm nervous, but what I do hear goes like this . . .

'Smart. Yes. Strong. Wow. I like that. Angry . . . *hmmm* . . . determined . . . with an attitude problem . . . outspoken . . . I see . . . powerful . . . *bossy*!' This is easily the closest I've ever come to having that wrinkly old talking hat sit on my head from that Harry Potter book. She feels about some more, squashing and squishing and grabbing . . . how does she *know*? She touches my nails.

'Nail varnish,' she says, which sounds like she's smiling, 'but it's layered. Glitter, I bet! And you're clumsy, it's chipped . . . and impatient too . . . it's smudged, you didn't wait for it to dry.' I blush, even in the darkness. 'Some are bitten. That's a bad habit. You like colour. I like that.' She pinches my fingers.

'Ouch!' I yelp. 'That hurt.'

'Sensitive, a worrier. But a warrior too. In both senses of the word. You are a little worrying warrior.'

I quite like that myself. I grin in the darkness, but then I quickly collect my smile up. There's still plenty of time to murder me, I suppose.

'Either you live near school or you're lazy, and your parents are overbearing crybaby bumpkins or you have incredible balance. Which one is it?' she demands.

'I'm sorry, what?'

She grabs my wrist, almost stopping my pulse. 'Just answer the question.' She says this sounding almost fed up, as if I'm the one wasting *her* time.

'Can you say the options again, please?' I spit nervously.

'So you're not *sharp*. I should make a mental note of that. OK. So do you live near school? Are you lazy? Are your parents crybabies that don't let you out of their sight, or do you have incredible balance?'

What does she even *mean*? I pause to think.

'Don't you dare take your time,' she orders. The torch balances in her mouth, or at least I think it does.

'Let me help you. Your balance isn't incredible, as I *felt* how you climbed up the mats.'

I dip my head in shame. I mean, I know I'm not the most *agile* of girls but *really*? That stung. Can you feel shame in the dark? Yes, I guess you can.

'Your parents can't be *that* overbearing because you're here, staying the night at school, so they aren't over-protective. So it's not that. You are not lazy, otherwise you wouldn't have bothered to climb up here in the first place . . . so . . . so' – she clicks her tongue, she likes the guessing game – 'you live close to the school!'

'I don't,' I say softly, and she freezes in surprise as I continue, 'I mean, I don't live far, but I don't live close.'

'But . . . so how come you don't have worn-down calluses on your palms from gripping the handrails on the bus like everybody else?' She seems genuinely curious.

'My parents drive me or I walk.'

'You *walk*?'

'Yes. Often.'

'Can I feel your hands again?' she asks.

I give them to her and she feels her way around them again. I begin to relax.

'I say . . . *this*.' She begins to rub my finger, as if her hand is a rolling pin rolling out a bump in some pastry. 'What is this?' She touches the hard nobble on my finger. 'A disfigurement of some kind? A lost bone?' I know what she's talking about. The same *wart* that got my granny in a pickle.

'Writer's bump . . .' I sigh, half embarrassed and half proud. I feel, for once, like an expert at something. A mini-mayor of a town naming a hill for the first time: 'This shall be known, from this day forth, as Writer's *Bump*.'

'Writer's bump? *Bump? Writer's bump?*' She says it proudly, letting the word live on her tongue, like a child learning a new word. 'You're a writer. Yes, of course.' She tugs some more at my bones individually. 'You are creative and artistic. You see the world through unique eyes that no one else can see through. You are . . . you are one of a kind. You are quite special.' She jumps up. 'You . . . you *have* to be my friend . . . you weirdo worrying warrior, Writer's Bump!' And at that moment she turns the torch on her own face. 'And I am Leila.'

Leila.

It's all too dark for me to see properly, but I do see a flicker of the longest most beautiful golden hair that I have even ever seened . . . like in an actual way, like as if her hair was made of shredded-up gold fibres; it flashes about like butterfly wings. She really *is* the princess at the top of the pea bed.

'Well . . . come on . . . we've got work to do.' She starts to urgently boot me off the mats.

'Work?'

'Yes. Of course. You don't think I came tonight to eat teeth-rotting grainy candyfloss and watch interpretive dance about endangered species, do you?'

Probably not. 'I don't know why you came here, I've never even seen you before,' I say defensively.

'That's *your* fault for not spotting me.'

'So, do you go to this school?'

'Yes, of course.'

'And how old are you?'

'My body is thirteen. But my mind is ageless.'

'And what work is it that we have to do?'

'Get my bow and arrows back OBVIOUSLY.'

OH. OBVIOUSLY.

Once we are out of the gym cupboard I can get a proper look at Leila. She isn't wearing pyjamas like the rest of us baboons. Unless she goes to bed in complete ninja combat gear. What a REBEL. At first sight I like her already. No, I don't just like her. I LOVE her.

She is *cool*. It's as if Leila had been created in a computer game where you could physically build your dream main character: ninja on top; sporting a black Catwoman-style leotard. Safari combats on her bottom – a pair of fitted grubby beige shorts with scattered bulging pockets. A builder in the middle, with a canvas belt cluttered with various interesting complicated accessories dangling off it. And then her face and head: pure true, elegant, butter-wouldn't-melt *princess*. A complete contradiction.

Her legs are *artwork*. Splattered in scrapes and bruises, cuts and scabby knees. This is a girl that likes to get stuff *done*. And then, pulling the whole outfit together, a pair of beaten-up big black dompy boots on her feet. The shoelaces straggling, rotten and tired.

Hands on hips, she sizes me up. She must have caught me sussing her outfit out. 'And do you always wear curtains?' she smirks.

The plan was *semi simple*, she said. The most tricky bit was because it was Mr Fisher that confiscated the bow and arrows. He is the science teacher, and science is actually Leila's most best subject. He very cleverly hid the arrows himself and gave the bow to another teacher, so that meant we had to retrieve *both* parts of the device.

'Mr Fisher is a clever man,' Leila tuts. 'He would have anticipated my break-in! But I think I will be able to rescue it. With you on lookout. It's very fortunate we met.' She fixes her buttons, as if preparing for battle.

'So which teacher has the bow?'

'Mavis at Reception.'

GREAT. Of course.

At first it seemed like an OK idea to do this, mostly because I knew we wouldn't be able to get away with it at all. But suddenly the plan began to formulate quite impressively. If anybody could pull this off, it seemed this Leila could. Not being big-headed, but Mavis really did like me, and getting the arrows back would be as simple as convincing Hector that bogeys were the main ingredient in pesto.

But I couldn't steal back the bow on Mavis's watch! She had been so good to me. I couldn't do that to Mavis. What if we got caught and she got in big trouble at school and lost her job for being careless and gullible? What if she cottoned on to what I was trying to convince her to do and she lost all respect for me and ratted on me to the Head? Or worse . . . just looked down on me for ever . . .

Aarghhh . . . But equally, Leila was so cool and I wanted to be liked by her; I wanted to be *like* her! I wanted bished bashed-up knobbly knees and safari shorts and a torch and to be able to know somebody's entire personality by the touch of their hands. I wanted to hang out on top of mats and have cascading long healthy sparkly blonde hair that obviously wasn't brushed but didn't seem to tangle. I wanted the guts to be able to *use* a bow and arrow, let alone STEAL one back!

What a dilemma.

What would Will do? *What would Will do?*

No. Not Will. *Will's not here, is he though, Darcy?* Will's not here and he's not here for you. It's not *what would Will do* ANY MORE . . . it's: *what would* Darcy *do?* That's right! Dare I plunge headfirst into the swimming pool of risk, or do I play it safe and run up to the bit where you can eat chips and watch the risk-takers swim in the swimming pool of experience? Currently I stand on the perimeter of indecisiveness, my bluing toes curled over the edge, shivering.

I hadn't yet told Leila that I knew Mavis reasonably

well as that would narrow my choices. I decided to keep it to myself that she fed me sugary tea and I read her stories and sometimes we ate cheese-and-pickle sandwiches and shortbread.

Leila was still hatching a plan on how we would get the bow back. 'Science lab first, for the arrows,' she said.

'But how will we get in? The science lab is locked.'

'Yes, I know,' she says, all knowingly, 'but it's never stopped me before.'

'Have you broken into the lab *before*? That's so . . . *naughty*.'

'Duh! All the time. I have to have access to the labs, like in case I want to do some experiments or research . . . you know . . . steal the odd chemical, you know?'

No, I don't know, but OK.

On the way up it gave me time to think of what to do about Mavis and the bow. And if we were caught we could say we were lost. Or something. *Lost?* In the building we go to five days a week? Just follow Leila, Darcy, and *shut up*. You're being brave and cool and daring and you've made a new friend who thinks you are good. Try not to ruin it already.

The lights in the rest of the school were mostly off. The silver squares from the windows silhouetted onto the shoe-trodden and chewing-gum-polluted carpets, clawing odd shadows of the trees from outside, printing disfigured illusions onto the wall and floors. Leila sprang, hot-footed, up the stairs. I couldn't even hear her steps as she sprinted up cat-like. Sometimes I couldn't even see her at all. I thought that would be a good excuse, if I needed one, to say I got lost along the way, but she wouldn't buy that and would lose total respect for me. Equally I didn't want to lose Leila. She seemed like the sort of girl that would be tricky to find again, but all I had to do was wait for the shimmering angelic glow of her long flowing hair to get me back on track again. Now I really *was* a thief in the night.

The emptiness drowned my ears out. I was so used to charging down these busy halls, my shoulders knocking against the force of the older kids, the backs of my shoes being stepped on by some idiot not looking where they were going, and tripping up, falling into the back of the person in front, shyly apologizing.

I was used to the clatter of lockers opening and shutting, the shrill of evil laughter that makes you think every joke is about you. But then came the memories that made me happy: jokes I had with Will, the belly-crippling bending over. The small waves with Maggie as we passed each other on our way to lessons, like bus drivers going in opposite directions, honking horns. Sometimes people noticed me in school as *that writer girl*, and strange kids would look at me that bit too long or with that extra bit of interest. Not happy. Not sad. Like how a dog looks at you. Just kind of *looking*. Not now, though. Now, the corridors of school felt scooped out like Halloween pumpkins and seemed to go on for ever.

'I am going to show you something *amazing*, Writer's Bump!' Leila whispers, and then she whips off the buckle of her belt, rams it into Mr Fisher's keyhole to his lab, tugs and clunks the lock round into the worn brass keyhole, and then it clacks and opens, whining as if in pain.

Leila winks and slots the buckle back onto her belt, sighing with pleasure. She is unbelievable.

Like two shadows we slip into the science lab. Leila's boots smack on the lino floor and it sounds like tiny clapping hands. Leila confidently bangs a few lamps on as if the lab is her bedroom, and the rest of the room is still in darkness and quiet and instantly I feel like I was in a museum in a film and it feels truly outrageously good. I should write a story set in a museum. Another time, I think.

'Look.' She beckons me over. 'Look at this.' Leila stands over a big glass cabinet. Inside are what look like rocks and stones.

'What is it?'

'Fossils.'

'Fossils? Of what?'

'Of anything and everything. Anything can fossil. Sea creatures, plants . . . it's amazing.'

Without hesitation Leila finds the small key for the cabinet and opens up the box. It reminds me of when Hector was a tiny baby and I wanted to show him to Will. But he would be sleeping. I would stand over his cot and gently cough and nudge him to try and stir him out of sleep. And if he didn't wake up then,

I would just put my arms right in and lift him out. And even though I knew it was a naughty thing to do, it's only because he was my brand-new perfect baby brother. And I was proud and he was beautiful. And I wanted to show him off.

Leila is like that with these fossils, and she begins carefully lifting them out of the box and placing them in my hands, telling me to fill my fingers into every gap, reeling off information about each piece. She doesn't even speak in a whisper any more – it's like she doesn't care if she is heard or not, as though this information is valuable and important and the more people hear it, the better.

'I love them.' She looks down into the case. 'I could just spend hours in here with these fossils.'

'Well, I do quite a lot love dinosaurs,' I say back with pride, just also trying to showcase the fact that we have absolutely heaps in common.

'Yeah, I *suppose* dinosaurs are good, but it some-times gets on my nerves that people think they are the only things that become fossils. Some of my favourite fossils are from underwater stuff. It's not *all* about dinosaurs.' I feel a bit embarrassed in front of Leila because she speaks so frankly and stern, but I know that I shouldn't take offence to her. I know she only wants to educate me and broaden my mind.

'And . . . well, I guess . . . anyway . . . I mean . . . what idiot would invent one of the scariest most terrifying creatures in the world like the T. Rex and then stick tiny arms on it?' I offer, and we both begin to laugh in the science room. I decide to lighten the mood and begin to do an impression of a T. Rex, toppling things over with my tiny arms, and I frown my eyebrows. 'Wait till I get my hands on you . . .' I giggle, 'if I *ever* get my hands on you.'

Leila holds her tummy and laughs. We then lock the cabinet. I sort of wish we only came to the science lab to look at the fossils.

'When we're not in the middle of a massive mission, I will tell you all about the moon and the planets. About space. I am obsessed with it. And then if you like, I can tell you all about crystal and coral too. I think nature is amazing. Well, the universe in general, to be honest.' Leila stretches, and her hair falls like feathers. I watch her, her eyes X-raying the room. She is a chick on a mission.

'Now, where are MY arrows?' She narrows her eyes. She flips through the cupboards at crazily rehearsed speed, like a skilled magician does with a deck of cards. She rummages some more, hopping effortlessly up on the work surfaces – it is like watching a ninja in action, leaping across the room, then at times like a wild animal, shuffling and truffling.

'I don't know *why* bows and arrows aren't allowed in school, anyway.' She hops across the desks. 'They were only wooden arrows – they couldn't *kill* anyone . . . well, not *really*.' She jumps down beside me. 'And even IF they did kill somebody it would be a quick death . . . WAHHHCCCHHHOOOO!' She mimes the firing of an arrow and then pretends to be the shot person too. I laugh. 'I think Mr Fisher did it just to spoil my day. Him and me don't get on, we don't always see eye to eye.' She runs her hand under the desk. 'BINGO!'

'Are they under the desk?' I am amazed.

'Yes, he's taped them there. He's a clever man, Mr Fisher. But I am cleverer!' Leila unpeels the tape, kisses her arrows. 'My babies! Aren't they beautiful?' she asks me. I hadn't really thought of a wooden arrow as *beautiful* before. Still, beauty is in the eye of the beholder . . . or *arm* in this case. Leila tuts. 'He is such a silly man, that Mr Fisher, he should make better enemies than me!'

'Why don't you get on?'

'Because I know *my* kind of science, I know what I want to know, and if it's not what I want to know then I don't pay attention. He doesn't teach MY kind of science. So I teach myself. And that's why I'm better than him. I'm better than my history teacher too. When we are learning about kings and blood and gore and heads being chopped off and affairs, then I care, but when it's not . . . I don't. I lose interest. I fall off the learning wagon. And then it's really hard to get me back on again.' She starts rubbing her chin as though she has facial stubble. 'Mostly because the learning wagon is really slow and I'm on the adventure motorbike or whatever. Do you know what I mean?'

Funnily enough I do.

'What's your real name, Writer's Bump? I'm sure you don't have Writer's Bump on your birth certificate.'

'That would have been awkward if I'd grown up to hate writing. It's Darcy. Darcy Burdock.'

'Oh, whatever. Go home with that cartoon character name.' She nudges me, I blush.

'Shut up!' I elbow her back. 'No, that really is my name.'

'No wonder you were hiding in the gym cupboard with a name like that.' She shakes her head, raising her eyebrows, and I giggle.

If Olly Supperidge had said that I would be angrosawing his face into a set of garden furniture, but for some reason . . . I am not offended by Leila.

'You know what, Darcy Burdock?'

'What?'

'Darcy Burdock is *such* a writer's name.'

My heart flaps. I can hear it. Fluttering away nicely. Beating against my cage of ribs. There we go. 'Thank you.' I put my hands behind my back shyly. If you cross your arms it means you are uncomfortable, and I don't feel like that with Leila.

'Right. Halfway there.' She salutes her own head with the arrows. 'Before we leave we have to cover our tracks. Quick, use the sleeve of your curtains to rub away all our fingerprints. I'd HATE for us to get this far only to be let down by sloppiness.'

I don't know how I feel about Leila just now referring to my entire outfit as *curtains*. I watch her sniffing about, as though she is searching for clues.

'Do you really think Mr Fisher is going to test the cupboards for fingerprints?' It's doubtful.

'I don't know, but I never put *anything* past a madman. And I sure ain't gonna stick around to find out.' She LOVES the drama of this, I can tell. In her brain, she is robbing a bank, stealing jewels from a palace, breaking into a detective agency with confidential files.

Crawling downstairs, which personally I *don't* really think we had to do – but I think Leila just really loved to be crawling right this second because it made her seem extra-sneaky and extra-purposeful – I follow her, her grubby shorts and bruised legs and strands of hair winding their way down the darkened halls. The school doesn't feel like the school I know any more; it feels mysterious, exciting, an adventure land. I think I could learn a lot from Leila.

'So . . . Writer's Bump, tell me about yourself.'

'Well . . .' I pant. I am on all fours, trying to keep up with her animalistic scamper across the floor, my curtain pyjamas aren't nicely shimmying across the floor like her action attire is but I get with it anyway.

'I'll ask questions and you answer, that's more fun.'

'OK.'

'Parents . . . how many?'

'Um. Two. You? Where do you live? What year are you in? I've never seen you before and the school is so big, but I honestly don't recognize you—'

'This isn't about me, Writer's Bump. Who is your best friend?'

'Will.'

'Where is he?'

'Probably downstairs with everybody else.'

'Siblings?'

'One brother and one sister.'

'Pets?'

'One. A lamb.'

At that point Leila stopped, turned round, grabbed me by the wrists, stopping any movement of blood and said in a deep firm voice, 'You have a *lamb*?'

And I said yes.

'You're pretty much the coolest girl alive,' she hissed as if annoyed, but I knew she meant it nice. It was like angry passion voice.

I pretty much am the coolest girl alive, am I?

'Where are we going now?' I whisper.

'To see that old Mavis at Reception. I've never spoken to her, have you?'

AARGH! What do I do? It was going so well, all this me-hanging-out-with-Leila business. I don't want to ruin Leila's plans but I don't want to get Mavis in trouble. It isn't Leila's fault that the school curriculum is so dry and flat and uninspiring and she doesn't learn about the things she wants to, and it isn't lenient enough to let her carry a bow and arrow into school. But then again it would be a massive obese lie not to tell Leila that I know Mavis, because I do know Mavis, quite well.

But before I can say anything, 'Nope' popped out of my mouth.

'Didn't think so. Which means we will have to stick to Plan A.'

'What's Plan A?'

'Smack Mavis over the head with a brick.'

'*What?*'

'OK. So not a brick. But what about a book?'

'Leila. Leila, you can't.'

'So what do you suggest? Have you got another plan to make her move from her perch?'

Oh. *What do I do?* I like Mavis. But I like Leila.

'Is there no other way to get to your bow?'

'I don't know where she's got it hidden, so no.'

And then it hits *me*. Not a brick. Or a book. But an idea.

'Leila, can you get me a pen and some paper?'

'Why, what you got in mind, Writer's Bump?'

'I told you a white lie. I do sort of know Mavis.'

'THAT'S why I wasn't allowed to whack her with a brick!'

Chapter Eleven

'Wee hen!' Mavis looks so happy when she sees me that it does a bit fill me with guilt, but at least I'm saving her from getting smacked over the head with a brick. Would Leila actually do that? I just don't know.

'Hi, Mavis.' I smile. I'm not gonna lie, I was quite pleased to see her.

'What's all that you've got there then, lassie?' I am holding a pile of lined paper.

'That's what I've come to talk to you about.'

'Aye?'

'Yes, aye . . .' I can't believe I just dropped the aye bomb as if I was a fluent Scottish person. Awkward.

'Yes. I've written a story . . . and I mean, I know it wasn't in the schedule for tonight's, you know, activities . . . but I wanted to—'

'Read it! For everybody! In the hall!'

WHAT WAS I THINKING?

I am watching from the wings of the school hall stage. The first thing I see is Will (dressed head to toe in football gear, sweating his face off and still kicking that stupid ball. His ankle is all floppy, and his face is just so confused). Trust me to be looking for him for all that time earlier, and when I *least* want to see him, I notice him straight away.

As the music stops, the clip-clop of Mavis's high heels clapping over the wooden floor of the hall pierces the moment, awkwardly followed by a dismal dreary sigh, as it seemed the fun was stopping for almost a moment. And it was. And it was *all* at my expense. Will let the battered football he had been kicking patter to the ground. Bounce. Bounce. Bounce.

There is an audible groan as Mavis picks up the mic, taps it with her rose-coloured nail and says what anybody who isn't used to holding a microphone says when they are about to talk into a microphone: 'Is this thing on?'

Followed by an ear-bleeding scribble of feedback.

'Hello,' said Mavis. 'Some of you may know me from the Reception.'

The room tuts. The clouds of burned popcorn smell begins to waft over us, sobering the event. Making us all, but mostly me, feel like idiots.

'I'm the wee one that organizes all your paperwork.

That sort of thing. I do know a few faces.'

Those *few* faces she recognized dipped their heads in shame. Nobody wants to be seen to be hanging out with a teacher. But you couldn't not like Mavis. Even if you wanted to not like her.

'So. I know this is a bit last minute, and I know you're having lots of fun with the music and the costumes and the hot chocolate and hot dogs, and it's all very exciting and I'm certain we are raising lots of money for charity. But I wanted to give you all a wee surprise.'

Some people laughed. They obviously didn't know that *wee* in Scottish didn't mean urine either.

WHAT AM I DOING? WAS I CRAZY? DO I REALLY want to READ in front of all of these people? My heart begins to thud. My legs turn to syrup. It feels as though all the nuts and bolts and screws that fasten my bones and joints together are unhingeing. I am falling apart. Becoming clay. Soft. Gooey. Floppy. My throat is filling up with a thickness. Like sludge. Like butter. My breath is short and tight. I can't get enough air in my lungs no matter how I gasp. My toes are ringing, my hands are sweaty. And in my tummy, not butterflies but millions of flapping wild birds.

Aarghhhhhhh. *What am I doing? Why am I doing this?* I don't know who I am! Why am I helping this Leila, that girl I've only just met? Why am I assisting her in *crime*? At first it seemed like fun, but now it just seems stupid and weird and evil, and it all becomes too real. I am about to humiliate myself for *what*?

I start to suffocate in my chest. My lungs feel heavy, as if the bottom of them is filled with treasure. I can hear Mavis winding down; she is bigging me up now, telling them all how great my writing is. And how *special* I am. Yes, I am special indeed. Pretty special at being absolutely *bonkers*. I won't do it. There are big kids there – the *old* ones – and I am going to ruin their party. I am going to be the neeky geeky weird goody-goody that has to spoil everything with my childish lipsy little *feel sorry for me* and *I love education* story, while meanwhile I am the disguise for an evil hideous plot. Oh no. Now I need a big poo. My tummy feels like it is going to fall out. I have to calm down. I put my hand into the pockets of my curtains, close my eyes and breathe in deeply.

Be calm.

And then I feel something small and papery in my pocket. I pull it out. It is crinkled-up yellow notepaper, the same as Granny has in her diary. She must have left it in there from the measurements she was writing down when she was making my pyjamas. I open it anyway. And inside, in her firm handwriting, is:

Little Miss Burdock,

I think you will look just great in these pyjamas. Now I know we don't always see eye to eye, but I do have a soft spot for you deep in my heart, and you remind me of your mother when she was your age. Have yourself a lovely time at the sleepover and remember, don't talk to any boys.

Love Granny

X

Oh, Granny.

I put the paper back in my pocket and step

onto the stage. YOLO. I guess.

'Hi,' I sort of say into the microphone, and I think I hear Olly say something like *NO WAY* under his breath, but I can't be sure. And the next few minutes are a blank as the room leaps under a thick blanket of pin-drop silence and I read this thing I had just written moments before.

I think about Dad. How I wish I could help him. Inspired by the fossils. And by Leila, the amazing creature that has just invaded my life out of nowhere like some strange mythical dazzling bewildering beast, and how all those ideas had smushed together right under my nose to form one story. You never need to search far for inspiration when you recognize that it hides right under your nose all the time . . .

> Saskia's dad owned a museum. They lived on top of the museum. It was a terrible museum that nobody ever visited. The fact that nobody ever visited *and* the fact that it was so terrible just made Saskia love it even more. Even though it made her dad quite upset that it

was always empty, she enjoyed lurking in the weird hallways, ogling the strange curiosities, with only the sound of her feet cracking on the creaking floorboards for company. While her dad spent his days pulling his hair out, thinking of ways to get more people to come to the museum and how he was going to pay his bills, the worry bags under his eyes were big enough to carry a year's worth of potatoes inside (money was so tight that Saskia had to get her granny to make her a pair of PJs out of the old curtains as she had outgrown all her other ones!).

'It's because our museum isn't *themed*. All the best museums in the world are themed. We need to focus,' her dad would say while pacing.

But Saskia peered at all the glass display cabinets. Nothing matched up, nothing made sense. There were odd bits from the war, rusty jewellery,

even a full bottle of champagne that
was found at the bottom of the sea
from a shipwreck! There were yellow
teeth, yes REAL ones, that looked like
half-chewed-up bits of popcorn kernel.

There were skeletons of raccoons, cases
of butterfly wings and beetles that
sparkled when the light hit them,
jars of frumpy jellyfish and strange
containers of weird things that
looked like bubblegum floating on
oil. There were dusty mountains
of books of ancient
artefacts, worn maps of
magical lands and spyglasses.
Wonderful shoes and dresses worn by
famous-ish local people and huge derelict
beehives, pressed flowers and brass
shields. Even a sword! There were
paintings and footstools, goblets,
tea sets and old gramophones, hunks
of coral and precious stones. All of it

beautiful and special. But none of it seemed to draw in customers, and those who had visited never seemed to revisit. It was so strange – not even their stuffed big brown grizzly bear could attract visitors.

'What do people like to see in museums?' Saskia's dad asked her, sipping his 59th tea of the day.

Saskia glugged from her 5th cup of *mostly milk and four sugars that had just felt the bitterness of the teabag for 0.2 seconds.* 'Dinosaurs.'

'Dinosaurs!' her dad chuckled. Even in the worserest moods he always managed to conjure up a small smile for his little girl. 'And where am I meant to find dinosaurs from?'

Saskia shrugged, but in her brain she was thinking and thinking of what she could do to save the museum.

That night, her dad fell asleep at his desk, his face in a pile of bills and scary letters telling him he owed lots of money, money that he didn't have. Although he was asleep, his face wasn't rested. His forehead was a field of wrinkles and worry lines, his eyebrows were frowned, his eyes crinkled up like old sultanas. Saskia wrapped a blanket around him and stroked his head and turned his lamp off. Instead of going to bed herself she crept very gently downstairs to the museum. Her bare feet slapping against the wooden floor. Her eyes squinting in the darkness.

She could smell all the smells that reminded her of home; the cedarwood to keep the moths away, the swampy clog of old dust, the sour stench of damp and then the overriding smell of the polish that Dad used to keep everything shiny and clean. Shiny and clean for nobody to appreciate. Every time Saskia wandered the museum she found new things, bits she hadn't seen. The certain shine of a silver teaspoon, the hundreds of colours blended together in the wing of a stuffed bird, the saddened expression of the lady in a painting. Perhaps the museum just needed shuffling about? A revamp? A renovation? She had suggested the idea to Dad before, but he defended himself as usual, explaining how long he had spent arranging the layout of the museum, when really perhaps he just didn't like change. But change was a good thing, wasn't it? They could paint the walls? They could do a launch party? Perhaps she could carefully, VERY gently switch things about, and perhaps if she took her time Dad wouldn't even notice, would he?

I stopped at this point to look up, and to my surprise . . . everybody was listening. The room was so quiet and all I could hear was the crackle of my own voice, the occasional cough and then a 'shhhh' from someone else, annoyed at them for interrupting me. Then Mavis sighed, openly enjoying the story, hanging on my every word like Tarzan in a jungle of vines. I thought about Leila. Had she managed to find her bow yet? I checked to see how much of the story was left. I breathed in and continued.

Saskia decided if she was going to safely move everything around that she would need to plan it. Dad was a planner and it was something he took very seriously. She knew he would support the move more if he knew she planned it properly. In Dad's store cupboard she rummaged about for paper. What she was really after was that *big* stuff, you know, a giant big piece that she could impressively roll out like a scroll, like how the captain of a ship does when they plan what island they want to invade. That would *really* get Dad excited.

But her eyes were distracted by a very large box. She had to stand on a chair to reach it; she tried tilting it down to peep inside but the box was too heavy to lean. She had to shuffle the box inch by inch and it was heavy. Even if she managed to get it off the shelf she still wouldn't be able to bring it down. Standing on the chair, one hand balanced underneath the box to hold its weight, the corner of the box wedged against her waist and chest, she delved her free hand inside. First she felt the rustle of sugar paper and tissue paper, then of bubble wrap. She loved bubble wrap, and even if inside this box was just nothing but pointless pebbles, she would be grateful for the abundance of bubble wrap to pop later on in bed, she loved popping bubble wrap. Then she felt something cold and hard. A stone. And then a few more. All wrapped up, in different shapes and sizes. She began to bring the rocks out and carefully place them on the nearest surface closest to her. This lightened the box and made her able to bring it down to the floor so that she could have a proper look.

Under the glow of the proper light she saw that these were not any *stones*. These were *fossils*. Fossils of plants and sea creatures, shells and animals. There were so many.

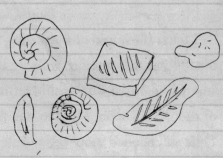

Hundreds. *Why weren't they on display?* They were beautiful and in such good condition. They all had a sticker underneath saying what they were. Saskia was excited – she could see herself spending hours inspecting the grooves and moulds of the fossils and trying to imagine how they were formed. This would make for a perfect new exhibition at the museum. OK, *sure*, it wasn't *dinosaurs*, but it was a new collection: one that would attract school visits at least! Her dad would be so proud when he saw them all displayed! Saskia would make posters and invite everybody to the launch of the fossils. Dad could learn a bit about each fossil and perhaps do a talk about how beautiful they were.

I felt a bit stupid about saying the word 'beautiful' but I think I got away with it. Fingers crossed. I'm sure Clementine won't mind letting me know if I did or didn't very soon. I had to stay focused and read on. Leila still needed more time to steal back her bow . . .

Saskia spent nearly the entire night researching each fossil. There was so much to learn but it was quite easy to identify the shapes. Most of them were very common. She had been taught by her dad about the grooves and marks of a fossil when she was very small. Who needed dinosaur fossils when there were all these?

But there was one tricky one that she couldn't find information for. No sticker underneath. Nothing at all. This was the most beautiful fossil of all. A pearly stone one that twinkled when the light hit it. The shape was curved and crinkly, like scales. She knew that experts knew more about space than they did about the bottom of the ocean, so this must be from down there, from a bit that nobody knew anything about.

She held it close. It seemed warmer than the others but it had been sitting in her warm hand for a while. She was getting tired now too. Her eyes were slowing shut and her brain had turned to custard-like slush. This was her

239

favourite one by far, and not just because it was, in her opinion, most lovely, but it had a special magnetism that drew her towards it. She had a fascination with it that made her not want to be apart from it. She needed to go to bed. In the morning, with fresh eyes, she would be able to work out what that fossil was. Do some research on it.

But for now, she took the fossil with her to bed. It was small, and there was no reason why it couldn't fit underneath her pillow, so that way she could dream into it all the hopes she had of it changing her and her dad's life. She snuggled up with her polar bear teddy, Ozzy, and fell into a deep, well-earned sleep.

I think I hear a couple of snorts at this mention of the teddy bear. See? I told you, didn't I? Why does EVERYBODY have SUCH a complex about needing a teddy bear to snuggle? It's normal, you know. I try not to let it unsettle me. My hands begin shaking. I breathe.

Saskia was dreaming the strangest dream.
She was in the desert. The hot sun barked
in her face and she squinted; beneath her
bare toes was the furiously baked sand, the
dunes continued for miles behind. The heat
was so intense it was like a hot hairdryer that
was blowing into her face, and she loved the
sunshine but this was a new heat. She heard
the roars and growls and groans of something
unusual, something that she had never heard
before.

She ran through the sand – it was difficult,
like riding a bicycle on the highest gear. Plough,
plough, wade, wade. The ground beneath her
changed, shifted, turned cool into fresh plush
new grass. A thick carpet of the stuff. The air
was moist and wet and fat with dewdrops and
humidity. She heard the peeps and squeaks, the
cackles and laughter of creatures whose calls
left her bewildered. She couldn't understand
them or make them out. The flicker and flutter
of what seemed to be wings, the hum and buzz

of what seemed to be insects, rattling closer and closer to her face. She put her hands up to protect herself from the rapid hovering but these were new sounds that sent her brain spiralling and the buzzing got louder, louder than any electrical appliance.

Water, suddenly, beneath her, and dense thick haze. Churning, turning, rolling, a mist, a dense moist mist, no, a fog. A swamp. A lagoon. It was dark. The moon shone. The water was thick and sludgy as though it was made up of minced-up slugs and lizards. She saw the ripples of scales in the water, something splashing in the water, a claw, reaching for her, closer and closer and closer and closer and closer . . .

Saskia woke to the clatter of Dad being his usual upside-down self in the morning. No doubt the kitchen would be a mess of dirty pots and pans, and by the sounds of things he had overslept and really needed a strong cup of tea before he would even think about attempting to open the museum. Not that it made any difference. Still nobody would pay a visit. Saskia stretched in bed and Ozzy tumbled out of the bed and dropped to the floor. Rolling over, she spread her arms out and groaned, and her bones creaked as her fingers fanned out, then she remembered the fossil underneath her pillow. She searched for the stone. Maybe Dad, now that he was awake, would help her identify the fossil . . .

But it was gone.

Frowning, Saskia sat bolt upright and lifted her pillow up. Yes, the fossil was small, but how could it have *gone*? Vanished? She had held it in her hand until she had gone to sleep, but that was when she saw the burned black hole in her mattress. Only small, the size of a fried egg. She went to touch it, and it was still warm. Grey ash responded to her breathing and danced about on her sheet, and a charcoal crust fell away into her fingers as a spiral of white smoke floated out of the hole. The

hole made its way through the entirety of her
mattress, so that she could see her carpet,
on the floor, in full view. Like a mini burned
trapdoor to the floor. She was a curious girl,
and some wouldn't, but she *did* push her hand
right through the cindered hole in the bed. She
shuffled her hand about. *No. Nothing.*

She sat up again. It sounded obvious but
perhaps she was still asleep, trapped in a
dream. It wasn't unusual for her to dream of
the museum because of all the strange oddities
and happenings that they were used to. It fed
her brain regularly, stuff to chew on in the
night; exactly the sort of ripe ingredients that
dreams needed. But this felt too . . . real
. . . too . . . exact. And not dreamlike at all.
Rubbing her eyes, she stood up, and that was
when her bed curved. Lifted like a hill. As if
a mole had just dug down into that tiny hole
and created a mound beneath her. She was
suddenly thrown off the bed and onto
the floor.

By the time she flicked her hair out of her eyes she saw what could only be described as a giant purple lizard underneath her bed, its back pressing into her mattress, its long arms and legs, its yellowing claws, and its shiny thick leathery skin, ribbed in scales. *No, she was dreaming, this couldn't be real.* She counted to ten. One. Two. Three. Four. Five. Six. Seven. Eight. Nine . . .

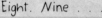

She pinched herself.

She slapped herself around the face. And again. But the beast was still there. It was bigger than her bed. Its arms

and legs alone were the size of her. But its head
. . . if it had one . . . was tucked away. She
gently shuffled forward on her bum, closer. She
grabbed her shoe as a weapon. Thankfully Dad
believed in *sensible* shoes, so it was nice and
heavy. She practised using the weight of it in
her hand. It could do some damage to perhaps
a goldfish, but it wasn't going to take down the
purple monster under her bed.

Closer and closer she crept forward, on her
knees now. The purple skin was the realest
thing she had ever seen, tough and
ridged. Like snake skin but thicker.
Not wet but shiny, glossy. Then she
saw what seemed to be an extra
leg but it was covered in stiff black
ridges. Sharp. Like a fence, and the
end of it came to a point,
like a spade. A tail. This
thing had a *tail*. And
just when her brain was
adding 2 and 2 together to

make 376, the head of this enormous bewildering creature spun round, lifting the weight of the bed with it, opened its spiked toothed jaws and let out a flume of bright orange fire. It set the curtains alight instantly. And Saskia's future set of PJs went up in flames.

The dragon then turned to Saskia, who was too afraid to scream, its blue eyes softly reflecting her reaction. The dragon hiccupped a polite little burp of smoke, closed its eyes again and fell back to sleep. Leaving Saskia, panting and sweating from the blaze, panicking about how not to let this beast set the house and museum on fire.

Gently sliding out, desperately not wanting to wake the snoring creature, Saskia crept out of her bedroom. It seemed that today the floorboards were extra creaky, *obviously* (always the way, whenever I am trying to sneak

247

downstairs to steal a biscuit the floor always creaks more than usual). Once the door was firmly shut behind her she ran down to her dad as quick as she could.

'Dad!' she called towards the kitchen, scrambling in — her socks seemed to slide about on the waxy wooden floors . . . 'Dad!' she called again . . . but he wasn't there. Clutching onto the banister, she slipped down the staircase, still calling for her dad. Through the museum, past the stuffed bear, the glass boxes of butterflies and shiny beetles, the mummy. Until she saw him, with the box of fossils. He looked sad, worried and anxious.

'Dad?' she asked. 'Are you OK?'

'Where did you find these?' he asked. He sounded cross — that kind of cross when you are trying to stay calm and not show you are cross but that you really are.

'I-I . . . was looking in . . . I-I-I . . . was just trying to . . .' Saskia had never seen her dad like this.

'Trying to?' He considered her for a moment.

'To save the museum,' Saskia gulped, her hands behind her back, her eyes on the floor in shame.

'Well, I think you might have!' Her dad's face lifted into a smile. 'We can do an exhibition on fossils! We've got so many here! We could do a *whole* season!' There was Saskia thinking she was in trouble . . . but she wasn't. Her dad was over the moon. But she had to tell him about the dragon sleeping under her bed. What would he say then? Though she had never seen him this happy, this jumpy and excited.

'Dad. There's something I have to tell you—' she began.

But before she could continue, she heard the sound of footsteps. Unusual footsteps that she didn't recognize coming from behind her. Her dad's jaw dropped, his eyes growing in size as the shadow of the dragon fell over Saskia.

'Morning, guys, can I get something to drink? I have a tickly throat.'

And at that point Saskia's dad collapsed.

'Pathetic,' the dragon said. 'I'll have to make my own coffee, it seems.'

Saskia spun round. 'But you're a dragon . . . and you like coffee?'

'Well, of course, frothy coffee. You know, the one where the milk is fluffy and the chocolate dust sprinkles go on top?'

'A cappuccino?' Saskia offered.

'Whatever. I wonder why it surprises you more that I drink coffee rather than anything else . . . there is a talking dragon before you and that's all you can think to ask me.'

'How can you talk, then?' Saskia asked the dragon, her hands on her hips. She stood like a warrior. She wasn't going to show any sign of weakness in front of this dragon, not while her dad was unconscious – well, not ever.

'What a boring question. How dull,' the dragon tutted.

'OK, why don't *you* try asking *me* a question then, seeing as you're so interesting?' Saskia rolled her eyes sarcastically, still calling the dragon's bluff.

'Very well.' The dragon sized her up. 'Why are you so short?' he huffed.

'Short! I am not short! Nobody *ever* calls me short! I am only twelve but I'm over five foot five!'

'You're short compared to me. I'm tall.'

'I am tall too. For a human girl.'

'I am tall for a dragon.'

'I've never met a dragon so I couldn't say.'

'But you can say we have *something* in common.'

'I guess so.'

'What's your favourite food?'

'Hmmm. Chocolate and ice cream.'

'No way!' The dragon went to high-five Saskia, except he had four claws not five fingers. 'Same here!'

'Really?' Saskia was not convinced by this coffee-slurping, tall, chocolate-and-ice-cream-eating dragon that popped out of nowhere and set her curtains on fire!

'Who *are* you?' the dragon asked her.

'WHO AM I? WHO are *you*, more like?'
Saskia replied with confidence.

'Who am I? Well, how dare you . . . I've
lived here far longer than you.'

'Well, that's just not true, is it? I have
lived here my whole life and I have never ever
seen you around before. Ever.'

'And now we are *both* here, see? That's more
things in common. We are basically twins.'

'Hardly.' Saskia narrowed her eyes.

'I like you.' The dragon grinned.

'Why?'

'You're peculiar.'

'Says the oversized fire-breathing purple
lizard!' Saskia's tongue spoke before she could
think.

The dragon spluttered with amusement. 'You
are witty.'

'Where did you come from?' Saskia asked;
her brows were still frowning.

'*Please*. Don't pretend you don't know.'

'Not from the fossil?'

'Of course.'

'I don't believe it.'

'How boring. I thought you had an imagination.'

'It is *quite* hard to believe.'

'Not really. *Somebody*, and now I'm assuming that SOMEBODY is *you*, took me out of the box, warmed me up and here I am.'

'I took you out of the box, but I wouldn't say I *warmed* you up.'

'Did you put me in your pocket? Hold me in between your grubby hands? Bake me in the oven?'

'I don't think so . . . all I did was . . . put you under my pillow.'

'There we go. It warmed my blood. It woke me up.'

'That box was full! Will the same happen with the other fossils?'

'No. Only mine. My fossil is different.

My fossil has a heartbeat.'

'I don't believe you.'

'If you don't believe me, then how did I arrive here, and if you didn't think I was special, then why, out of all those other fossils, did you choose me to take into your bedroom and hide under your pillow? You couldn't put me down, could you?'

The dragon was right; Saskia knew there was something magical about this fossil. 'Now what do I do with you?' she said.

'You mean to say . . . how do you put me back inside the fossil?'

'I didn't say that!' Saskia looked embarrassed, she tried to gobble her words back up.

'I've only just this second got here, and already you want me to leave? We haven't even got to know each other properly. And just to think . . . I was going to help you.'

'Help me? Help me, how?'

'No, no, don't you worry about it, you just

get on with your . . . *coffee-free lifestyle*
and stupid . . . I don't know . . . collection
of weird bits that nobody wants to visit that
basically just takes up all the space.' The
dragon folded his arms (I don't know if you've
ever seen that happen but it looks ridiculous).

'Are you a genie? Like a genie in a lamp?
One that grants wishes?'

'I beg your pardon?' The dragon looked
insulted. 'Have you seen what a genie looks
like? That fat old round belly? Those ridiculous
eyebrows? Those obscure revolting piercings? That
terrible ponytail and unfashionable goatee? I
mean, seriously, if we are *ever* going to maintain
a friendship, *honestly* . . .'

'I don't know what you are.'

'I'm *not* a genie, I can tell you *that* much.
Besides, the main difference, other than the
obvious, is that the genie isn't free. I am free.
Sure, I am bogged down by my fossil, but once
I am released . . . I can do what I like . . .
but just once . . . and just for a day.'

Saskia eyed the dragon up. He was so tall, bigger than the stuffed bear by far, like two or three fridges balanced on top of each other, or a whale with legs. And his skin was so scaly and shiny. His eyes were big and glassy, his nostrils alone were big enough for Saskia to fit her foot into, and his mouth could . . . his teeth could . . . her heart began to beat faster.

'I won't be eating you. Don't worry,' the dragon mouthed in a crackle, and even though she couldn't trust this dragon — Saskia didn't know what it was capable of — it did make her feel slightly more comfortable, and she let out a deep sigh of relief.

'So what are you going to do on your one day of freedom?'

'I *was* going to help you.'

'How?'

'Coffee first. Then business.' The dragon stretched. 'Being crunched up inside a fossil doesn't do *anything* for the spine, I tell you.'

They tell you, at school, when you're reading out loud that you must not talk too fast, that you have to breathe, that you have to look up every so often. They tell you that it's to communicate with the audience, that eye contact is really important and precious, but I think it's really so you can check that the audience are still listening, that they haven't fallen asleep.

When I can finally take my eyes off the page, I look up. To do just that. To see if anybody is listening, to make sure they still care and are paying absolutely loads of attention. That even though I can sort of see their bodies from over the top of my page, that they haven't just switched off, leaving me to read to an empty hall of no ears.

But they are all smiling.

'What does the dragon do next?' a voice shouts from the crowd. I can't quite make out who it was that shouted it, but I really blush. I look into the thick crowd of people. I can't even make out Clementine's curls, which is a good thing, as no doubt her moose face would be cradled in the halo of hair with a big unimpressed smirk wiped across it. I go back to reading, as I've got this far, and I just hope that by now Leila's got the bow.

I hope my story wasn't too babyish. Lots of bigger kids are in the hall and my mind very quickly began to drift. It felt like I wasn't reading any more, like my mouth was speaking, motoring away, my lips moving, my tongue clicking and clacking, but my brain wasn't there. It was taking a back seat, chilling. The words were melting and merging and morphing into one another on the page. I kept trying to sail back into the moment, but my head was being stubborn and I was floating away, imagining all types of things like what everybody was thinking when they were looking at me. Next I imagine that there are two of me and one of me is reading and the other is in the crowd. How would I react to some weird little girl with knotty hair spontaneously reading a weird story about a museum and a dragon in the middle of what was meant to be a party. How would I feel?

I think I would feel quite jealous of that girl.

I continue . . .

'I feel like a new dragon.' The dragon smiled after his coffee. 'That hit the spot. Why don't you drink coffee?'

'Because it tastes like blended-up monster poo. No offence.'

'None taken. Has your father woken up yet?'

'Yes, but he's in bed, he thinks he dreamed he saw you, like you are a hallucination. Really, I just think he's tired. He is under a lot of pressure. He is really stressed.'

'Why is he stressed? Are you a naughty girl?'

'No! Well . . . I don't think so . . . It's the museum. We have no money, and nobody visits . . . sometimes it makes Dad a bit snappy and shouty. He doesn't mean to be mean and grumpy, and then he feels bad and it makes him upset. Do you know what I mean?'

'Yes, of course I do. We have work to do.'

'What sort of work?'

'We have an exhibition to announce.'

'What exhibition?'

'Let's see, what did you have in mind?'

'Fossils. I was going to display the fossils, that's how I found you . . . before you . . . you know?'

'Ruined everything?'

'Not exactly.'

'Sweetheart, I *saved* you! Forgive me, but who in their right mind wants to come into a boring old building to look at a bunch of rocks?'

'I thought it would be interesting.'

The dragon chuckled meanly. 'Oh dear,' he sighed. He was waiting, his claws rapping on the floor. 'Are you ready?'

'I think so.'

'Then this is what we are going to do . . .'

Saskia made posters and signs, she called the press and the reporters, and in no time at all a long queue of eager visitors was coiling round the walls of the museum in anticipation. The journalists were banging on the museum door shouting the name of Saskia's dad. He got up from his bed and peered out of the window and saw the eager, excited people. He was *hallucinating* again, he had to be. He hadn't seen a line of people outside his museum since . . . well . . . ever.

'What's going on?' Saskia's dad panicked. He could hear the rumble of people from outside, and the flashes of cameras were blinking even through the window, coming through the crack under the door.

'Dad, just get washed and dressed!'

'Washed? *Dressed?* What for?'

'Just do it!' Saskia yelled. 'Trust me!'

And off he skidded. He wasn't going to argue with his daughter, and leaving the museum in her hands clearly wasn't the wrong decision.

'Are you sure you want to do this?' Saskia asked the dragon, who was sipping his last coffee before the show.

'Saskia, not too long ago I was trapped inside a sad old stone. Look at me now, drinking coffee . . . *hanging* with you!'

Saskia blushed. She grinned bashfully. 'Thank you,' she whispered.

The doors opened to the museum, and
the people gasped and snapped pictures. Arms
of microphones grew like flowers out of grass,
reaching out towards Saskia. Despite her height,
Saskia felt taller than ever, proud and excited.
Her dad, at this point, in his (two sizes too
small) blue velvet suit, which *had* certainly seen
better days, flew down the staircase.

'What is all this? What are we doing?
What's going on?' The words rolled out of his
mouth.

'We're saving our museum.'

With the building full, the museum heaving

with visitors, and a new crowd bustling by
every minute, the exhibition was ready to open.

   Everybody was in suspense. People had heard
the rumours, but was it true? Did the museum
really have a *dragon*?

   Saskia's dad wasn't convinced, and he
began to bite his nails. He had got used to the
emptiness of the museum, so he began to back
out . . . he wasn't sure that this was what he
wanted, but then . . .

I don't know what came over me, but I had got
so into the telling of this story, the concentration
and warmth I was feeling off my new audience was
boosting my confidence and my energy somehow. I
wasn't expecting this level of enthusiasm. Even though
I had written this story, I think there was a strong part
of me that never really saw me actually reading it out
loud, in front of people, especially getting this far . . .
I don't know, but I thought somebody might have told
me to shut up by now but they hadn't.

   I am not sure what provoked me . . . but I put my

paper down. Gently. Gently. And
spoke directly from my imagination,
to the room . . .

But then I see Clementine standing
in the crowd. All of a sudden. She
does not look happy. She keeps looking
at the faces in the audience, seeing if
anybody is enjoying my story. Looking
for a companion to roll her eyes with.
My voice trembles.

The dragon entered the room.

The room went silent, and a few people
fainted as Dad had done when they first
laid eyes upon it. All were too shocked to
take pictures, but some had their cameras out
videoing the entire thing. Some men and women
screamed, children cried, some 'wowed' in
chorus. The room was electric with reactions.

The dragon winked at Saskia before he let
his huge victorious wings drop down and span

open, soaring him to the ceiling. He was swirling and dancing in the sky. He could *fly*. He was *flying*. Round and round and looping and hurling and reeling and scooping and ducking and twirling.

I felt my hands motioning the actions, I could see the dragon in my head clearly now, I used my fingers to demonstrate to the crowd, my facial expressions moved to act them out. The audience laughed loudly.

Saskia's dad could not believe what was before him. He rubbed his eye sockets, looking at the audience who were 'ooooohing' and 'ahhhhhhing' and clapping and cheering. The dragon circled down to the ground, his claws clicking on the floor, and the people stepped back as much as they could, but the museum was so packed that this was difficult.

The dragon stood tall, opened his mouth and spoke. This was when the drama really happened and people began to lose control. Here was a talking dragon. A dragon, talking. This couldn't be true. But it was.

Saskia stood back, proud.

'Ladies and gentlemen, boys and girls, what you have seen today is all 100% real. I am sure a lot of you have questions about who I am, how I came to be. I am a dragon. As you can tell. I was inside my fossil and then this charming, wonderful, witty, clever girl found me and gave me, other than coffee, a sincere breath of life.'

And then . . . I can't believe it. My eyes sting from the horrible borrible NOribbleness of it.

Clementine, the fungus, out of nowhere, shouts, 'GET ON WITH IT, DARCY. IF WE WANTED A STORY WE WOULD ALL READ A BOOK!'

I can't believe it. I guess the story was dragging. I flush blush bright orange, red, purple, blue even.

Mrs Ixy comes marching over but before that can happen, old Mavis has jumped on the old mic, hasn't she.

'How dare you? You nasty little so and so!' Mavis hisses. 'What makes you think you can say those unpleasant words!' I think Mavis might cry, in fact she's getting so mad on my behalf that I don't even need to be that mad myself now.

'Look, I don't mean to offend you, secretary lady, but a lot of us have ACTUALLY rehearsed for this show so . . . it's kind of *not* fair that Darcy just rocks up and gets to do some story she's just made up.'

'It doesn't matter if you spend a moment on something or fifteen years, *whatever-your-name-is*, talent is talent. You've either got it or you *don't*, and *this* is a talent show, is it not? And Darcy has *got* talent, wouldn't you say so, guys?' Mavis asks for the room to react and the awkwardness is numbing silence until everybody spills into a giant ear-clustering 'YES!' and then . . . as if I'm some sort of actual world leader, people begin shouting, 'Carry on . . . carry on . . . carry on . . .' But I think that's because not everybody knows my name. But at least I wasn't called 'whatever-your-name-is', hahahaha.

Clementine sulks. Her hands on her hips. Pouting.

267

Snarling. Kissing her teeth, as the room begins to tremble. I think actually people do just enjoy the sound of lots of people saying the same word at the same time in a loud voice, whether that's the word 'Darcy' or 'dog poo', but I'll take it. I gulp. Breathe. And continue.

The dragon pointed to Saskia, who in response flushed a deep beetroot colour, while her heart sang.

'A breath of life so that I may exist and meet you all. People think that fossils are boring. That they are dull. Bits of boring old rock that would perhaps only interest . . . I don't know . . . a small puppy that would only do his or her business on top of them . . .'

The dragon grinned at Saskia; she tried not to laugh.

'But they are not. They are the footprints, the heartbeats and souls of what was. Fossils are our marks, they contain history, they are what we have left behind. They are wonderful.

They are precious. And do *NOT* believe it
when anybody tells you they are anything but.'

Saskia felt her heart melt. This dragon
had got under her skin, well and truly. The
reporters and journalists began squabbling, taking
photographs, scribbling things down on their
notepads.

'This museum has an exhibition *all* about
the wonder of fossils, and as of today it will
be open. I urge you to go. You'll be pleasantly
surprised. I came from a fossil, remember.'

The dragon then, as a finale, blew his
big beastly fire breath just enough so that
the flames kissed the cheeks of everybody in
the room, but it did not burn them. He then
launched up and flew away. The crowd went
nuts. People were screaming, cheering, clapping
and crying. Rubbing their eyes in utter disbelief.

Saskia's dad stood at the museum's exit,
where he pre-sold hundreds of tickets to the
fossil exhibition. Waving everybody goodbye and
saying lots of 'see you soon.' The three words

he had wanted to say to his visitors for so long, because he knew these people *were* going to come back.

When the museum had finally emptied out, the people had left for the night (people were *camped* outside in the hope they might catch a sight of the dragon once again), Saskia's dad swept the museum floor while Saskia made the dragon coffee in the biggest mug she could find. She couldn't wait to see him and say thank you. She didn't know he could *fly* the way he did!

She carefully bounced up the stairs, not wanting to spill the hot coffee on the floor or burn herself. 'Dragon! Dragon!' she called. 'Dragon, that was *amazing*! I've made you coffee . . .' She hurried into each room, the coffee splashing over the rim of the cup, leaping onto the ground. 'Dragon . . . Dragon?' she called, scampering into her bedroom, her little room. How long ago it seemed she had first met her new friend right here in this very room,

when it was just that same morning. How this
dragon had changed her life.
   But she saw or heard nothing.

A somehow deeper silence drank the room up. I
felt emotional speaking the words out. I don't know
why. It wasn't because of Granny. She left us when we
weren't expecting it, but I didn't know Granny. Was
it because of Pork? I don't think so because we could
still visit him whenever we wanted and Giorgio was
so nice AND he had a pizza oven. Was it worrying
about Dad and how we have no money and how he's
stressed and sad and angry? Was it my nerves?

I was slipping into the moment. I wanted to stop.
I wanted to cry. I wanted to get up and run away and
go home and see Mum and Dad and Poppy and
Hector and Lamb-Beth and Uncle Adrian. I didn't
want them all to cheer my name. I wished I'd stopped
when Clementine suggested that I did. Why did I carry
on? Clementine was right – this wasn't even a finished
story. Where did this sudden confidence come from?
What made me think I could just jump up and read

this? I hadn't even watched any of the other performances! But it was too late, we were a team now. The audience and I. Leila and I. I had to carry on, but . . .

What happens next? What happens in the story next? What happens next?

'What happens next?' Will shouts out. 'What happens next, Darcy?'

Will. My mouth, without me even thinking, opens up once more.

But the dragon wasn't there. He was nowhere to be seen. There was no way she could have lost him, he was so big.

'Dragon?' The coffee spilled onto the floor a little more and some of the brown liquid burned her hand a little but she didn't feel the soreness of it. She rested the mug on her bedside table. She knew it was pointless because he was so big, but she crept underneath her bed, back to where she first met the dragon. Her hands stung. The ashes were still there from where she first met him, but so was his fossil.

Why was his fossil *there*?

She picked it up. It was hot. No. He couldn't have. No.

She shook it, touched it, held it close to her chest. It was piping hot. She wrapped it up in her jumper. 'Dragon?' She saw her own eyes reflected in the shine of the fossil's crystal, and right back she saw the eyes of the dragon in the fossil itself. 'Are you there? Dragon? Please, talk to me. I made you coffee . . .'

The eyes inside the fossil winked at her and then they faded away.

'No!' Saskia screamed as the fossil's temperature became cooler and cooler and cooler, the colours of it smoky and dull, but still bright, in its own special way.

Saskia held the fossil close. Tight. She cried hard into the fossil. So hard like she couldn't breathe.

> She saw the burned curtains, charcoaled and
> destroyed, the ashes the dragon had left behind.
>   And it was done.
>   The dragon had gone home after living for
> one day. Less than even a butterfly.

My own voice was drowned out by the sniffles and gasps of my audience. I couldn't say any more. I saw Mavis's tears drip drop onto her blouse, and even the candyfloss man gently wiped away his tears as they plopped into his mixing bowl. Jeez, candyfloss is meant to be sweet not salty, mate . . . I felt guilty. I had made people cry.

'It's not a sad story!' I shout. 'The dragon . . . was within her,' I said. 'He was within her. The dragon was her fight, Saskia's fight. It's her strength; people still came to see the fossils. The museum was a success. It's a happy ending . . . guys? It's happy.'

And then everybody bursted into an applaud.

Chapter Twelve

I didn't realize strangers liked to say well done to other strangers so much. I think for a lot of people it was the firstest time that they've ever even acknowl-edged me. I was completely overwhelmed by the amount of 'well done's I was hearing in my ear that I forgetted what *well done* even meant any more. It was hard mostly to shake Maggie off, who wanted to show off to everybody that we were friends. And I wanted her to show me off, just not now when I had to go and catch Leila and see if she got her bow back.

'Darcy, that was *so* good and so brave. What made

you suddenly leap up and do that?' Maggie asked, her face full of pride.

'I just . . . I don't know . . . got the . . . *urge*, I guess.' Maggie's friends were all gathered round too; they are all arty types and so I think they appreciate my species.

'It was major *spontaneous* and *outrageous* and *daring*.' One of Maggie's REALLY hippy friends gripped me. 'I love that *random* stuff, when you just . . . you know . . . think . . . *stuff it*! I don't care what the world thinks, I am doing this for *moi*!'

Moi? Is that 'me' in French? 360-degree eyeball roll to THAT.

'I can't believe Clementine, she was so jealous. She is such an idiot,' Maggie sighed, shaking her head.

'I know, but I mean, she *has* been rehearsing all week,' I tried to defend her shyly.

'Yeah, but have you heard her sing? It's TERRIBLE! She is just annoyed because everybody loved your story so much. She forgets it's not a competition.' Maggie smiled. 'Speaking of terrible, did you manage to catch our dance? It didn't go down so well,' she murmured.

'It was *très* awks,' added the hippy friend, who I was

quickly realizing embroidered her personality with annoyingness.

'It wasn't that bad, was it, Darcy? The dance, what did you think?'

I didn't want to tell the truth to Maggie and say I'd missed her dance because I'd been trespassing around the school with this girl Leila I'd only just known for five minutes, looking at fossils and trying to steal back her WEAPON, and the only reason I read that stupid story out loud was to distract everybody. So I lie.

'Tough crowd,' I said, because I didn't know what else to.

Will practically skidded into me. 'Oi oi, superstar!' He *safed* me, which is basically when two friends put their knuckles against each other to mean *hi*. It's quite a lot like when dogs sniff each other's bums but less gross. Just another way of hugging except people can't spread rumours that you're in love. I've never been very good at *safeing* or *spudding* or *touching* or whatever else people call it. I have no navigating compass installed in my brain that tells me when I am too close or too far from somebody, like how a cat has whiskers so they know if their head will fit through holes and stuff. I do *not* have anything like that basically. *Instinct*, I think it is called. I could NEVER drive a car.

'What made you read like that? I thought you weren't going to!'

'I just got the urge,' I said again, just as I did to Maggie. It was my thing. An *urge*.

Next week on Channel Four, watch The Girl with the Urge, *a poor girl named Darcy Burdock who suffers with the uncontrollable urge to write and read stories in any circumstance, don't miss it.*

'It's weird, one minute you don't even want to come to the sleepover, the next minute you're only the blummin' entertainment!' Will elbows me in the side like we're in on some private joke.

'Yes, I know, weird. I know.' I try and distract him. 'Do you want to get candyfloss?' I point at the pink featherlike webs of cloud.

'Is something up?'

'UP?' I screech in the highest voice possible. If there was ever a *this is how the word UP's voice sounds like*, it would be that there, what I just did. I say, 'No.'

'OK, it's just you're acting a bit . . . look, it's not about Clementine, is it? She's so annoying, she's just so livid that you're so good and everybody liked your story, she is spoiled like that and can't be happy for anybody else. I bet she won't be allowed to do her song now, they will probably punish her for that! Honestly, mate, don't take her personally, she's just jealous.'

'No, I know that. I'm just nervous, after the reading. I just . . .'

'I understand.' Will smiles. 'It's one thing to read in front of everybody, but to read something you've written too is a total different ballgame. You smashed it, Darcy, honestly.'

'Thanks, Will.' I am not even appreciating anything he is saying, all I am thinking about is Leila. Come to think of it, I've not seen Mavis since the reading – where has that old thing skulked off to now? What if she's caught Leila in the act? All my efforts would be for nothing!

'You sure you're OK?' Will asks me again.

'Yes, I'm just going to . . . I left my . . . stuff . . . at Reception so I'm just going to . . . get that.'

'Cool, I'll come with you.' Will smiles again.

'Can I just . . . ?'

'If you don't want me to come, D.B., just say.'

'I do, but can you not' – how can I make this not sound rude or weird or suspicious? – 'come because Mavis asked to see me right after . . . just on my own.'

'What? Weird. Why?' Will isn't buying any of this, and he looks baffled. 'Are you in trouble?' Often when someone is naughty at school they are sent to the school office, which is where Mavis is, to then be passed on to see the Head. They are the *shoulders*, I guess . . . or the *neck* of the school, close to the Head but not quite the Head.

'In trouble?' I screech again. 'No! Why would I be in trouble?'

'Awwright, calm down. Nah, I get it, all the teachers are probs well proud of you and just want to big you up!' Will grins cheekily – he knows my temper, that's why. 'Hurry back though! Clementine is singing soon. I do NOT want to miss that!'

How could I forget?

'I'll be right back.'

I can already hear Mavis's voice cluttering up the Reception. It's such a musical voice; it makes you almost want to dance to it.

'Honestly, she is so special, such a lovely girl too . . . speak of the . . . there she is in all her glory!' Mavis looks beyond proud. 'We were just discussing how great your story was, Darcy. You always have those clever and unexpected twists and turns. Such an imagination.'

'I don't know about that, Mavis.' I blush; I can feel the teachers' eyes skinning me, their straight teeth like iron fences pushing me out a bit even. *Some* teachers have a weird business going on in their heads, I've noticed. It's a bit like they want you to be the most amazing you can be, but a bit of them is like livid that they aren't quite as magnificent as you. Not quite as *free*.

'She's too humble, is that wee hen.' Mavis drops her head, as though I am a cute baby duck paddling in a bowl of water. 'So proud.'

I can't see Leila anywhere. I try and peer over the top of Mavis's head to see if she's in the corner, on the naughty chair waiting to be told off, or standing facing the wall, which we sometimes have to do when we are bad but not as much as we used to have to in baby small school. Mavis is in too much of a good mood to have just told somebody off and to be planning punishment. When she has usually told somebody off she goes all achy and tired, as if the telling off has really taken it out of her, when really it's because she gets heartbroken that she has to do it. She likes to be happy all the time, mostly.

There isn't even any sign of interference, it's like nobody has even tampered with anything at all. The filing cabinets are closed. Maybe she backed out? Maybe Leila got cold feet, couldn't do it? Changed her mind? I decide to go and find her . . .

Before I knew it I had been around the entire school and Leila was nowhere to be seen, I had looked in the gym cupboard and all the classrooms were locked anyway and the lights were off.

And just when a sudden sheer sadness swallows me up I hear the cheesy snarling wail of Clementine.

'WAHAAHAHAHAHAAHHAHAHHAHAHH-

HAHAHAHAHAHAHAHHHAHAHAHAHAHAH-
HAHAHAHHAHHHHHHAHAHAHHAHAHA-
HAHAHAHAOOOOOOOOOOOOOOOOOOO
OOOOOOOOOOOOOOOOOOO!'

I can't help but run back into the hall. Clementine
must have been able to sing after all . . . what about
her being punished for trying to sabotage my reading . . . ?

Actually . . . on second thoughts, after hearing her
singing . . . perhaps this was a punishment after all.

For our eardrums.

'SO, curtain-wearing girl . . . how did it go?' Dad asked
as I got in the car next to him. It seemed he didn't hate
me *so much* like yesterday, which is good. Perhaps a
night off from one another was all we needed to heal
our bruises.

'Really fun!'

'So, you're glad you went?'

'VERY!'

'I've got to say it feels weird picking you up in the
morning, in your jimjams – there were some right

odd-looking nutters coming out of that building! Some people went to town on their outfits, eh?'

'Did I miss anything on my night away?'

Dad shook his head. 'Not much, but I want to hear about you! Still trying to work out how the school coped with organizing a sleepover. Did they lose their minds?' Dad laughed. 'What did you do?'

'Will and I hung out all night and drank hot chocolate, and Dad, there was even a candyfloss machine and a slush-puppy maker, I had mixed red and blue flavour . . .'

'Obviously,' Dad chipped in.

'Obviously.'

'And what else?'

'A popcorn machine and music, and even the older kids were all there and *even* a few people liked my curtain pyjamas!'

'Ah, see, told you, but *just imagine* the amount of compliments if you'd worn the *CRASH*, *BANG*, *WALLOP* ones.'

'Shut up, Dad! I had to wear those pyjamas, Granny made them for me.'

'Fine, I'll have the *CRASH, BANG, WALLOPS*. Give them to me!'

'You can *have* them! And something else . . .'

'What?'

'I wrote a story.'

'Yeah . . . *whoooop deeeeee dooooo*, it's far more rare to find out you *haven't* written a story!' Dad honked his horn but not in an angry driver kind of way and started singing a make-shift made-up song where the lyrics were something along the lines of: 'My daughter is so good at making stories up, she writes them . . . laaaa laaaa.' As you can see, *very* basic. I could really tell he was trying his absolute most hardest to be happy when he had worries on his mind, but that's when you know somebody loves you, I think, when they try and be happy for you even when inside they are a mess.

I play along – it's nice to see his smile – and in between giggles I manage to say, 'No, I wrote a story at the sleepover and . . . I read it. Out loud. In front of everybody.'

'What?' Dad nearly ran an old lady over walking two poodles across a zebra crossing. 'You did *not*?'

'I did!'

'No way!'

'Yes way!'

'NO way!'

'YES way!'

'And did they love it?'

I was shy, I didn't want to sound all showy-offy, but Dad knew my face too good.

'They did, didn't they?'

And I nodded and squealed.

'That's my girl! That's my Darcy!' And then he went back to singing his terrible but SUCH cute song as we wound home, elated.

But the mood did not carry on at home.

It was like the windows had not been opened for seventeen hundred several years. My home was a dungeon.

'Mum's . . . a bit . . . you know . . . it's organizing the funeral for Granny. It's been hard work,' Dad said out of the dark corner of his mouth.

I followed him into the kitchen where Mum was at the table. She had loads of disgusting scary-seeming forms all splayed out on the table, her hair was all raggedy and she looked tired. In the sink were piles and mountains of dirty washing up, all heaped and gross. This did not feel like a precious Saturday. I can't believe that just one week ago Granny was being sent off on a train back home and now she was gone. For good. It really was a one-way ticket.

'Hiya, monkey, how was the sleepover?' She reached forward for me, but it didn't feel like her for one second. She was forcing joy too. Squeezing it out like a fart that wouldn't pop out.

'Fine.' I smiled at her. I knew she wanted me to be *happy smiley in love with the universe Darcy*, but I felt worried and anxious. 'Where are Poppy and Hector?'

'Poppy and Hector are at Timothy's, thank goodness. Just had to get your sister out of the house for a bit! Her and Uncle Adrian did their own version of *Grease* last night. I am still scarred.'

I tried to laugh but I was jealous they'd had fun. I bet Adrian was the girl, Sandy, from the film. Sandy is one of the main characters in *Grease* and she starts as a terrible mighty excellent geekazoid who wears cardigans, and then at the end bursts out in a slinky all-in-one black suit. Mum said the suit was so tight that Sandy had to be sewn into it. So she's probably still wearing it till this day because she can't get out of it. I expect it stinks.

But I bet Adrian and Poppy's version of it was glitzy and great.

I felt guilty angry that I went even to the sleepover and had a fun time when all the while Mum was so sad and everything was so stressful. Even though it's the granny that died that we don't love as much, even though it was probably right that I was all out of Mum's hair and not being an annoying nit.

'Where's Uncle Adrian?' I sniffed the atmosphere

and all I smelled back was *tense*. I am NOT feeling this.

'He's gone to collect some of Granny's belongings.' Mum sifted through the paperwork and didn't even look up at me not even ONCE.

'Oh,' I said back.

Dad walked out of the room in a slow gentle patter. I wanted Poppy and Adrian to both be here, so I could tell them about reading my story in front of everybody and all about wonderful Leila and Clementine's heckling and wretched singing.

But nobody was here except bad and unexplainable news and feelings and all this paper on the table.

'What's all this stuff?' I pointed to the forms and paper.

'It's horrible forms. It's surprising how many forms there are to fill in when somebody dies.'

'These are all about Granny?' I scoop up Lamb-Beth, and she nuzzles into my elbow. I wish I was her. In her own little animal world.

'Sure. She had a long life. This one's for her bank and this for her doctors, this one is the dentist, another bank here. There's a lot of people and companies that you have to inform when somebody goes.'

'That's ugly.'

'You're right, it is.' Mum squeezes my hand and pats Lamb-Beth's head. I sigh.

'Because in this time people should just have to worry about being upset or whatever, and they can't because they have to suddenly think of that person that they love and miss so much like a number for a bit.'

'You're so clever, monkey, that's exactly what it's like. It's so frustrating because they all put you on hold on the phone for ages and most of them are expensive lines and nobody wants to give you any information because they need answers to security questions that I don't know the answers to. Honestly, it just goes round and round.'

'Are you getting a chance to be sad and miss your mum?' I ask her, not knowing or really wanting the answer.

'It's strange, because we didn't really get along. You know that, Darcy. I never really saw her. Our views were not the same. I mean, you know what she was like, Darcy, you know how old-fashioned she was.'

Yeah, she was basically from the prehistoric times, I am thinking. 'Is it because you were adopted?'

'No!' she says, almost shouty. 'I was very lucky to be adopted and be taken care of. But Mum didn't want me to do my art, she didn't want me to move to London. She didn't even like Dad at first.'

Well, not getting along makes SENSE. I don't like her EVEN MORE now!

'She also . . . didn't really *agree* with Uncle Adrian's lifestyle choice, and that was hard for us. She was just a very old-fashioned person. As I said. She knew what she liked and what she didn't, and when she didn't like something . . . she had to make it VERY clear. Regardless if it sometimes hurt people's feelings.'

'But you miss her, don't you?'

'In my own way. Anyway . . . I better get back to this load. I think you need to get in the bath, don't you?'

At least my family don't hate me any more, like how they did when I left them.

I run a big enormous bubble bath and try to enjoy my luxury day without *the kids*. I can't wait until Uncle Adrian comes back so I can tell him ALL about everything, but the seconds are moving more slowlier than the world turning. I need to cheer myself up. I hum a happy song. I let the water of the bath run right to the top while I take a clean towel out of the cupboard and fold it on top of the toilet. I try my best to fold it how they do in the hotels, with a little triangle bit folded over. In my head, I'm in one of those perfume adverts or chocolate ice cream adverts. Sometimes, I've happened to notice so you don't have to, they make yoghurt adverts the same as ice cream or chocolate adverts, trying to make the yoghurt seem as scrumptious as the ice cream or chocolate. So close your eyes when those adverts appear on TV . . . Don't be fooled.

The sun begins to shine through the window. Pure heaven, at last without any bothers. I dip one foot into the water. It's *BOILING*. AARGHHHHH. EMERGENCY! I immediately take my piping foot out of the water and sit, splashing about, naked, on the bath mat like an absolute water moose beast, slipping and sliding about. My toes have a little heartbeat. Throbbing. Ouch.

But now I've filled the water all the way to the top there is no more room to top up with cold water to Even Stevens it out. My only option is to wait until it cools down. That's not going to do. It's boiling hot so it will take ages and I am impatient. This is completely ruining my restful ME time, so much for peace and quiet time! My only other option is to sacrifice my arm and plunge my hand down into the water, release the plug and then refill with cold to balance the water out. They NEVER show THIS bit in the adverts.

Three. Two. One . . . wahhhhhhhhhhhhhhhhh.

'OUCH. OUCH. OUCH,' I say to myself as my

hand goes down, fumbles with the plug and pulls it up. The water instantly begins to gurgle and swirl down the drain and I bring my arm up, which now tingles and has gone an even darker rawerer shade of red than my toes. It is *pounding*. I cradle it. The blood fizzes. As the bath level goes down, I begin to let cold water in and I plunge my arm back in to put the plug back. Then I try and get back into the advert mode, even though the girls in those adverts would only ever look calm and elegant and beautiful. Not naked and covered in burned patches while the rest of you remains pale and freezing.

While the bath is refilling I get bored and pick up a bottle of shampoo. I begin reading the ingredients in the mirror, like I am the woman in the advert. Every time I mess a word up, I have to start again from the top. Some of the words are really tricky. But I keep going. I begin to dare myself – I have to finish the whole passage of ingredients without a single mistake, in a posh advert voice, before the bath fills to the top. But I keep getting all the words tumbled up and wrong. I keep going . . . s*odium laureth sulphate* . . .

'DARCY! DARCY!' It's Dad, banging on the bathroom door, and he makes me jump. I turn round. Water is EVERYWHERE! Spilling over the bath, the

cold tap furiously spouting
away. I scramble over and turn
it off, release the plug – the
bath is now freezing cold – meanwhile trying to sound
casual.

'Yeah?' I say in a normal-ish voice.

'You've FLOODED the HALLWAY!' he growls.

Chapter Thirteen

I think my dad might cry.

He doesn't. But he wants to.

'I'm sorry,' I say for the trillionth time.

Dad ignores me and continues to dot various saucepans and pots and buckets around under the hall. The water is drip dropping slurping through any gap it can morsel into. It sounds like.

PLINK.

PLONK.

DRIP.

DROP.

But depressed.

Not over the moon.

'I am,' I say again. Because I am. I didn't mean to flood the bathroom. Because Mum said it would be a waste of water if I didn't wash in it, I still had to wash my hair and heaps of suddy soapiness also starts funnelling out of the ceiling. It looks like an alien infestation.

'Darcy. Please. Just. GO!' he yells at me in that oh-so-shouty voice of his.

'Dad, I can help you.' I start trying to help. I scoop up loads of loo paper and begin unravelling it and laying it down on the mess to soak up the water. I want to help him, like how Saskia helps save the museum. If we just work together, you know, we can actually be quite a useful team, but I can feel his eyes on me. All livid. Wishing I didn't exist a bit. I hate this side of Dad. I carry on sloshing the toilet paper about. But the water is just too much and the tissue begins to fall apart and turn to gloop.

I try to hide it but Dad can already see the mess I've created. He is not happy. Not happy at all. We've still not heard ANY news whatsoever about him renovating the toy shop either so I assume he hasn't got that job. HUMPH. I try to help some more.

'Leave it alone, Darcy.'

'It's OK. It's my mess. I made it so I can tidy it—'

'GO!' he storms at me, and his shout strikes my heart and shocks me so much that I burst into tears, and he doesn't even care and neither does Mum, and this time they are actual real-life tears. Not crocodile ones. Not alligator ones. Not drippy water ones or ones you get from staring. Just actual unstoppable painful tears.

And all I hear is Dad shout to himself/the house, 'How can I afford a plasterer?'

Nobody comes to comfort me and my hair is so knotty and didn't get a proper wash because the water was freezing cold. The flooring of the bathroom is curling up at the edges but I don't bother telling Dad about that. I try to step across it and pad it back down with the weight of my body so he doesn't think he has to buy us a new bathroom floor too, but it doesn't work.

When my tears are all dried I take Lamb-Beth and

we go and hang out in the living room, all wrapped up in my witchy blanket, her purple and green pattern comforting me. I fold my fingers through the tassels and lie with my body on the sofa and my feet on the walls. Which I'm not meant to do, but my shoes aren't on so I just don't care. I impatiently hum a new song that I don't even know to kill the awkwardness. I can't BELIEVE I am already back to being most hated in the house. Then again, technically three members of the house are not here, so the chances are that the odds would not bend in my favour.

'Is there any chocolate in the fridge?' I ask Lamb-Beth, but she doesn't care, she is chewing her own ear. What an idiot.

I trudge to the kitchen. I can hear the pit-patter-pit-patter from the water still trickling through down into the hall into a saucepan that's collecting the leak. There isn't even *that* much water.

I don't know what the fuss is all about. The whole house smells like a big soapy bubble bath. It's actually medium to extra amounts of agreeable, if you ask me. I realize you didn't ask me, but technically you are reading this book so you are under some sort of contract to care about my beliefs all the time.

The fridge smacks its lips open.

Oh, Darcy, my fine young friend, good to see you again, it says.

(It doesn't.)

There is nothing inside. I wish Dad wasn't finding it so hard to get work. Then there might be something good in here. Then I could flood the bathroom whenever I wanted. The only bit of chocolate I can find has been there for probably one gatrillion years, but I pick it up anyway, unravel the gold foil paper. It tastes all particular gross and fridgey. Yuck.

I can safely say that I could really do with my brother and sister to come home and entertain me. I laugh to myself when I think of how I always like the idea of Poppy and Hector's company more than in actuality. Then I think that might be a lie. They are pretty sick. I can't wait to tell them about Leila, the weird and wonderful amazing girl that I met in the gym cupboard. How she turned up out of nowhere, and now she has vanished into absolutely nowhere. Like a dream. She is like a superhero. Flying in and out of my life. I think about my reading, replay it over and over in my head. I think about Granny. How moany she was. But then I feel a bit sad. Did she die all alone? Was she frightened?

I feel sad.

I wish I had somebody to talk to.

Holding Lamb-Beth, I listen in again to the droplets of water coming into the saucepan, Dad's angry grunts and stomps, Mum's turning of the paper in the kitchen.

'I'm not getting involved,' Mum keeps saying. Snide.

I am starting to sink into miserable sand, I am falling in, drowning in the sand of sadness for no good reason at all, and just when I think . . . ah . . . ah . . . ah . . . ah . . . ah . . . I'm falling . . . I'm falling . . . I'm falling . . . save me . . .

The window knocks and whose stupid face is there? Will's.

It's as if he read my mind.

That's a sign of real true-life friendship.

'Awwwwwright, mate?' he smirks as I open up the front door to let him in. 'Your neighbour Henrietta is a right nosy parker.'

'She's all right,' I say. Lamb-Beth winds round my legs when she hears Henrietta's name. Sometimes her and Henrietta's dog, Kevin, show off to each other. Well, when Kevin was nice, before he bit Sir Dusty Pork.

Will drops his BMX on the patch of grass. 'Can I come in?'

I realize then that I am completely barricading the door like a total security guard for some reason, just not wanting anybody to see the flooded hall, my sad mum, my stressed dad.

'Do you mind if we go for a walk?' I say.

'Course not.'

I put Lamb-Beth on her going-to-the-park lead and we walk round the streets I know.

Henrietta from next door lifts her blinds, rolling her net curtains back, pretending to fiddle. Kevin snarls when he sees Lamb-Beth, but howls as we walk in the opposite direction. I hear his groan through the wind.

Lamb-Beth begins to bound like the lamb she is. She is probably happy to be out of the house too. I wonder how SHE feels about not having to share our attention with Sir Dusty Pork any more . . . she *never* really had to share mine, to be fair.

Cyril, my across-the-road neighbour, is 'working out'. He is wearing a matching top and bottoms jogging kit and fast walking. He offers me a swift wave. I can hear tacky 80s power ballads screaming out of his out-of-date headphones.

Past the flower shop, where the woman with

the big chubby bum is wrapping up a lovely bouquet. She winks at me; she has a customer so can't say hello. I'm glad she didn't get too skinny and still kept her chub.

I walk past Giorgio's restaurant to show Will where Pork's true home is, but the restaurant looks closed for now.

Funny how life just still goes round.

I think about how all these people that I see all the time have no idea what *truly* goes on in my life.

And how I have no idea what goes on in theirs.

We just be nice to each other.

Because we do.

'I'm sorry about your gran,' Will finally plucks up the courage to say. I am not sure how he found out, as I hadn't really told anybody except for . . . but he steals the words out of my mouth. 'Clementine spread *that* gossip like a virus.'

Course she did.

'Don't be sorry,' I reassure him. 'You didn't kill her . . . or DID you?'

'NO!' Will shrieks, shocked that I would even suggest it.

'I'm joking,' I laugh. Will sighs in relief. 'It's not a big deal. Well, it is. But I didn't really know her . . . we didn't even really get on. It's not my best grandma.'

'Oh, that's OK then.' Will continues pushing his bike next to me.

Lamb-Beth is padding about and some strangers stop by to pet her. 'Is she a REAL lamb?' one of them asks. 'Or just like a dog that like *totally* looks like a lamb?'

'Of course she's a lamb!' Will snaps back at the stranger, and we continue walking.

I bite my lips so I don't laugh.

'I have a favourite nan and a gran that's just OK.' Will shrugs. 'I think that's normal.'

'Do you think everybody does?' I ask, wanting to feel less guilty.

'Definitely. Even though you're not meant to have favourites. Everybody has one. If you like them both the same, then you are lucky.'

'OK. That makes me feel better. It was so weird though, I couldn't even cry,' I say. More people point at Lamb-Beth. Sometimes I forget how spectacular she is.

'That's not weird. I remember when I was younger my mum's grandad came to stay with us for a bit, so my *great*-grandad, and he was sick so he had to sleep in our living room. He was so ill and so demanding and annoying. I clearly remember Annie and me just wanting him to get on with it so we could have our living room back. And even once he did die, Mum was just pleased that she could watch her soaps again in peace!'

'Oh, that IS bad!'

'I asked my mum why I couldn't cry and she said, "You're young and vibrant. You have so much to be happy about." And that was all. So I just carried on being young and happy.'

'It's the funeral soon anyway,' I huff. 'Another *event* to look forward to, I suppose.' I decide to move off the subject of death as things are getting a bit bleak and I don't like talking death with Will. Even though his opinion is valid. His mum is an angel now. So . . . 'The sleepover was fun in the end, wasn't it?'

'Yeah, but your story topped it for me! It was so cool. Proper sick how you just got up and read it.'

'Thanks.' I blush. 'Kind of wish we were still there, as my parents HATE me at the moment.'

'Why?'

'I just can't seem to do anything right. I just constantly manage to be annoying all the time.' At this moment Lamb-Beth decides to start a trail of lots

of little poos that look like identical to Maltesers in the street, as if walking a lamb on a lead around South London isn't already hard enough.

'Maybe they are stressed?' Will asks. I always feel bad talking about my parents with Will too.

'Yeah, my dad is waiting for this big job to come through and he hasn't heard anything. Until we do, we have to eat all own-brand cornflakes and use gross shampoo and it feels like all the things are coming at once. Pork leaving, Granny dying. And then guess what?'

'What?'

'I flooded the house.'

'Oh, you idiot.'

'I know. So, bad, isn't it?'

Will can't help but laugh.

'Don't laugh!' I say. 'My dad is well mad at me. There was soap and bubbles climbing down the stairs!' And I can't help but laugh too. Lamb-Beth throws me a look as if to say, HOW DARE YOU LAUGH AT THAT? But maybe it was just because I was distracting her poo. When we get our breaths back from the giggles I say, 'I don't know how to make it better.'

'Write them something? That worked for me when we fell out.' He nudges me and I blush.

'*Mayyyyyybeeee*. But will it just annoy them more?'

'No it won't.' Will scratches his head. 'Not if it's from the heart. If you proper mean it.'

'Hmmmm . . . do you think that will work?'

'Why don't you write something for the funeral? You could read it?'

'I don't think so.'

'Well, at least have a go.'

I clear Lamb-Beth's poo up and we continue walking.

'Black?' I don't have anything *black*. 'Do I have to wear black?'

'Yes, it's respectful.' Mum starts flinging through my drawers.

'But look . . . see if you can find anything that's black amongst all this . . .' I kick my wardrobe door. She hasn't yet mentioned the sincere state of my scruffy bedroom. Downstairs all I can hear is the evidence of Uncle Adrian, Dad, Poppy, Hector and Lamb-Beth having what can only be described as an absolute *whale* of a time. I didn't even realize whales have so much fun anyway. I am irritated. I want to go downstairs and play with them. I start to get a weird ANGRO-SAUR-US type of frantic frenzied lose-my-mind jealousy. *AGAIN!*

'How come they are just laughing and playing down there?' I sulk to Mum.

'Because *they* both have their outfits for the funeral.'

'I have my outfit for the funeral!' I yelp.

'Darcy, multi-coloured dungarees are not suitable. Granny wouldn't appreciate that.'

'I don't see why not. It's not – it's not like she's gonna *see* me.'

Mum tries not to laugh. 'You do have a point, but no, it's not appropriate.'

'But I love my colours,' I grunt. After getting through the sleepover dressed in my NOT ME pyjamas, I'm embracing my wardrobe like never before.

'I love your colours too, but please, don't be difficult today. Just make this easy for me,' she pleads. 'Now where's that black dress I got you last year for when you waitressed at Marnie Pincher's party? That's what I'm looking for.'

'I chopped it up and made it into little costumes to turn Poppy's Barbie dolls into Goths.'

Mum does a face to me that can only really be described as a full-blown snarl. 'Why didn't we do this before? We haven't got the time or the money to buy

you anything new now.' She is getting cross with me.
AGAIN.

'What are we going to do
then? Shall I just wear this?' I
point to my hot-dog onesie; at
least that's got bits of brown
on it.

'You can't even borrow
anything of mine; I only
have one black dress
too and that's my
stupid receptionist
outfit. What are
we like with all
our multi-coloured
parrot clothes? We are ridiculous.' Mum starts tearing
through my things.

'I do have these?' I point to the pyjamas that I wore
to the sleepover, the ones Granny made me with her
bare hands.

Mum scratches her head.

'I don't have a better plan, do you?'

'Not really, no. And I think that's actually not a bad idea at all. I think she would really like that.'

And all jokes aside, in all seriousness, I say, 'I think she would too.'

We start to attempt to put my room back together, and Mum resists the temptation to tell me what a pigsty it is, which I actually am impressed by, to be fair.

Mum huffs like she can't be bothered with her life for a moment and so it feels like a good time to say, 'Mum, I've actually written something for you . . . for you, and Granny.'

Chapter Fourteen

Dad is allergic to funerals. I think it's quite understand-able. It was a boring-and-a-half-long car ride away and we had to all squeeze into one car even though it's illegal, but Mum said she didn't care that it was. Dad and Mum sat in the front while Uncle Adrian, Poppy, Hector and me, wearing my pyjamas, squished into the back. Uncle Adrian demands that we pull

over IMMEDIATELY when we see a McDonald's Drive-Thru to get breakfast on the way.

'My treat,' he says to Mum, 'and don't look at me like that either. What's the point of working if you can't treat your family to junk food?' He smiles, and I am so glad he is here.

'But you're paying for everything,' Mum mumbles. Dad looks annoyed. I think his MANLY pride is getting knocked but he just needs to get over it. Dad normally pays for everything for everyone, so what goes around comes around.

Adrian tells us to order whatever we like. We are such naughty rebels these days. Uncle Adrian orders a McDonald's breakfast AND a bacon bagel AND an extra hash brown, a coffee AND an orange juice. 'When in Rome,' he comments, taking hold of the brown paper bag at the Drive-Thru. I don't get it. We are not in Rome. Unless he's been away for so long he no longer knows the difference between Italy and England. I don't like the breakfast at McDonald's because the sausage is a burger shape. It distresses my organs.

After the food we all regret it a bit because we feel all car-sickie and slimy and hot and troubled. Hector has spilled ketchup all down his shirt and Poppy is trying to learn lines for her school play, which is doing my head right in.

'Do the impression again!' Uncle Adrian keeps clapping his hands. 'Again, again, again!' He wants me to show him how Clementine sung at the sleepover.

'OK, it was like . . .' I hold one hand up in the air like I'm telling a dog to *sit*, and I stuff the finger of the other hand in my ear like I'm a diva harmonizing into a mic, my face all tightly squished up like I'm pooing out a poo the size of a watermelon. 'OOOOOOO,

WOOOOOOOOOOO, EEEEEEE, BABY . . . YEAH
. . . LAAAAAAAA, WEEEEEEEE, NOOOOOOO,
WOOOOOOOOOOOOOO!'

Uncle Adrian tips his head back with laughter, and
tears sprinkle out of his eyes. Real tears of happiness.

'Let's play a game!' I suggest, trying to make the
journey quicker.

'Yeah, let's play which car on the motorway you
would least enjoy to have,' Poppy suggests.

'Let's play sleeping,' Dad says, and closes his eyes.
That really means that it's best to just simply button
up and stare out of the window watching the cars
whooshy on by, the pollution-stained trees saying
'hello', the occasional misguided crow giving you the
death stare.

It's a cold day and Mum was right – everybody *is*
dressed in black. Most of the people are other nanas
and nannies and nans and grannies and grandmas.
How do you decide which one you want to be called?
There are so many choices. I might just go for a
different name altogether like *Cardboard*. My grandchildren will have to write my birthday cards like

'Happy Birthday, Cardboard.'

I am thinking this when it suddenly dawns on me how few people are at this funeral that I actually know or recognize. I really feel far away from Granny. I really realize that I never knew much about her, like what her favourite best cereal was, what her best planet was, did she pick her nose? How did she like her eggs? What her favourite books were, what did she dream about? I feel more guilty than ever.

In addition to wearing my PJs to the funeral, Mum has also made me wear these odd shiny shoes that make me look like I work at a bank. The worst thing is – I don't even know where they camed from. Shoes are one of those things that just sometimes turn up at my house and you know not to ask questions. Immediately when we step into the service I notice how slippery slidy the floors are. It's as if they have just been waxed that very day and I judder forward and slip, nearly knocking an old granny/nana/nan/grandma/whatever off her feet.

'Sorry,' I whisper, which echoes off the walls.

I wish I'd never agreed to read now, as this room

is so daunting and I don't know anybody not even, and all the herd of old people are sobbing before the service has even begun. I bet these people just come anyway. You know, for the social aspect – something to do, I guess.

'Let's sit here.' Dad ushers us into a pew, a quite nice long wooden bench. It's OK and I can sit down, which is good. My feet and calves and knees are wrecking, and because the floor is so slippery my muscles are completely exhausted from tensing them. I'm hoping Mum has forgotten about my reading, but then she says:

'You sit on the end, Darcy, so you can get up to read.'

Great. I don't want to read. I wish I never even wroted this stupid poem. I wish nobody ever convinced me. I wish I had at least shown somebody before. To get their feedback. What if it's absolutely horrendous? What if everybody laughs?

No. We are at a funeral, Darcy. Highly unlikely that there will be laughter.

And that is when I see the coffin that my granny is

deaded in. Obvs. I want to cry but I can't. I want to push tears out but they won't come. I want to cry just to feel, because that's what's *meant* to happen. Crying is what you're meant to do at a funeral, but tears aren't coming. Why? Am I a stone-cold evil bad person?

'Is she *just* there?' Poppy whisparks (whisper mixed with ask) Uncle Adrian. 'Just in that wooden box? Just like that?'

'Yeah.' Uncle Adrian nods. ''Fraid so.'

'Yuck,' Hector adds, quite rightly. 'Isn't she all *gone off?*'

'I imagine so,' Uncle Adrian says. I don't tell Hector off though because secretly I thoroughly enjoy gross things.

I can't quite believe it myself either. That Granny is just in a box. I watch it for ages. How do you go from one moment being alive, getting on trains, eating food, going swimming, watching TV and then just being in a box? I begin to feel shaky. Shaky and sad and achy and breaky in my heart. Then I start to think about my *I work in a bank* shoes and their slippery soles. What if I slip on the extra extremely shiny waxy floor when I walk up to the podium? And there's two big candles either side! What if I bump into the candles? Trip up . . . knock old dead out-of-date Granny out of her coffin and she falls out and she's all a zombie and everybody gasps and then hates me? What if I set the place on fire?

Oh no.

Oh no.

I can't read. When they call my name I just will not get up. I'll just pretend not to know they are calling me and will look as though I don't know what they are talking about. I'll tell Mum that I'm a terrified shy girl; she won't force me to do anything that I don't want to do. Will she?

The other old ladies are really crying now. I think they *came* to cry, because they are so TOO prepared with their little napkins and serviettes for tears. Do they even know my granny? I know nobody in this room other than the people I came with, so it really wouldn't surprise me. I think this is their occupation: going to other grannies' funerals and sobbing their eyes out . . . or perhaps they see it a bit like a hobby.

Like going to the gym or art class or something. It makes any tears that I did have brewing up instantly dry away because I don't want to look as though I'm just someone pretending to be upset and who enjoys crying my heart out either.

The slippery floor enters my fears again. Hector's shoes look like they have gripping on the bottom but his feets are so small. I would never fit in them but I still try and ask for them:

'Oi, Hec, pass me your shoes?' I whisper.

Dad frowns at me because my whisper echo-bounces off every wall.

'What?' Hector scrunches his face up to try and hear me.

'Pass me your shoes,' I grunt a bit louder, ignoring Dad.

'No,' he mutters loudly, 'you've got your own shoes.'

Everybody looks at us. If Granny were here alive my wrist would be pinched right now. Dad frowns again.

I look about. I AM WEARING MY PYJAMAS. Everybody else looks reasonable except me. I can see

Alice, my perfect second cousin who is my same age, on the other side of the room. She is with some other kids and they are snickering and talking and playing games on their phones. They look up at me and one whispers something into Alice's ear. It's obvs about my pyjamas, and I dissolve like aspirin in water. I bet they can't wait for my reading so they can laugh at me and be nasty. Why do I keep doing this to my annoying self? Why do I keep forgetting how much I hate this feeling? I can't read. I won't do it. I can't. I can't.

'And now Pauline's granddaughter would like to read a poem that she has written about Pauline and her own mother, Mollie.'

I shrink.

Mum leans over and pats me on the leg. Uncle Adrian squeezes my shoulder, and before I know it I am up, stepping as though I am walking on ice with butter strapped to my feet, so I don't fall over, inching over, my legs moving in squares, as if I am churning the butter with my ankles.

Hold on a sec. If I can read in front of my whole entire school a story that I just wrote to help a crazy stranger relocate her bow and arrows, then I can read a poem that I spent time on that came right from the right place.

A poem with meaning.

Yes. Every second reading it will be ghastly, but every second that is ghastly for me to read is magical for my mum. And my uncle. And my dad. And even my poor dead granny. I take a breath. And open up.

What is a mum?

My mum says that one day she was searching on the beach for seashells and then she stumbled across me.

I was a precious stone that she picked up, accidentally.

She talked to me every day inside her belly,

Read the paper, sung me jingles off the telly.

She waited for me like the summer,

She fed me up with milk and love,

She made me kind, she made me to⌐‚

She still gave love when there was

enough.

She said, 'Save that for when you grow up.'

And even that we were connected by an umbilical cord,

That wasn't the reason for the affection that I felt towards her.

It wasn't just because I was the first chick that she hatched,

It wasn't because we had the same eyes or that our blood type matched,

It wasn't because we laughed the same, had the same skin freckling,

It was something deeper, a certain kind of nurturing.

What is a mum?

It isn't always the person that cooks you up,

It's the one that cares for you and *brings* you up.

It's the one that gives you strength and confidence,

That cradles you in the night,

That pushes your hand into theirs and holds on tight.

It's the one that waits for you outside in a cold storm,

The one that calms you down.

The one that uses her big boobies to keep you warm,

And can tell you off by a simple frown.

It's the one that is your friend,

That teaches you how to love.

That never judges you for anything,

And does thoughtful things just 'cos.

She may not have made you in her tummy,

But she was there when you were teething,

And still you learn to call her Mummy,

Because a *mum* is a feeling not a meaning.

WELL, THAT WAS THE SCARIEST THING I EVER DID DO IN MY WHOLE LIFE.

Did I poo myself? I can't tell. But probably. Or at least a very heavy wet fart.

I don't see anybody crying, because my head is very down because I am so shyed out, but I hear so many snorts and sniffles and a particular feeling in the air. I can't wait to hurry back to my seat, not slip, and sit down and erase all those seconds. Cousin Alice isn't laughing any more.

Mum leans over with a shaky hand, clutching a wet snotty tissue and squeezes my own hand. Hard. Awwright, Mum. *Chill out,* I say to myself.

The man who was leading the service steps back up again and starts doing some more talking, to round things off. The whole thing is a mighty blur, to be honest. The man has a voice like a tumble-drier, just going round and round, being all roboty and not stopping – it's like we have wasps caught in our ears, and then Hector, really loudly, says, 'I'm bored, Dad, how much LONGER is this going to go on for?' And a few people snort and giggle, some tut and Dad *shhhhhhhh*'s him in *such* a serious tone. 'Can I have the keys to the car?' Hector continues, even louder, not taking the hint at all. 'I want to get out of here, go play with my McDonald's toy.'

Mum snatches the keys out of Dad's hands and gives them straight to Hector. He waddles out of the service, his gripped shoes slapping on the waxed floor in time with the jingle of Dad's keys.

When it's FINALLY all over, we say goodbye to everyone and people start leaving flowers and Mum gets all upset because she forgot to get flowers. (Well, that's what she says but I know it's becaused flowers are so expensive. Which technically must be illegal because all the flower person is doing is digging lilies and stuff out of the earth and charging £20 for them.) Even if you do get them from the woman down the road with the chubby bum, they are still expensive.

But it's OK. Because what she doesn't know is that Poppy and I have made six little bunches of bouquet garni. A little bouquet, using all Mum's garden herbs,

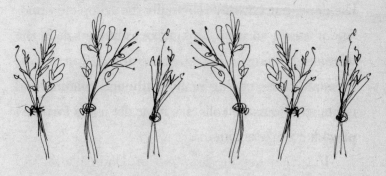

each the size of what a Barbie would use. They look terrible. Manky, squished together, covered in crisp crumbs from the bottom of Poppy's bag and falling apart, plus neither of us are good at knots or bows so we had to use hairbands, AND because we never can find any hairbands of our own we had to ask Uncle Adrian for some so they are all brightly coloured and sparkly, but I think it looks rather cheery.

'My girls,' Mum cries, and squeezes us in, and people look, which is proper embarrassing, but it is a bit cold anyway outside and her boobs are warm so it is OK.

Afterwards we have to go to this thing called a 'wake', which I really don't understand becaused if you even asked me, which, to be fair, I know nobody has done, but Granny is actually the complete opposite of *awake*, so it's a bit kind of rubbing salt in the wounds. It's boring here because it's all just people in small circles talking really softly and sniffling and eating cold sausage rolls. It's basically just a birthday party for all these nans.

Chapter Fifteen

I am back at school and I HAVE to say that I am truly delighted to be here. I have asked everybody in my school and nobody even knows of this Leila girl. I have been to the gym cupboard but it's always locked every time. Maggie SAYS she thinks she knows of Leila, and she is in her year, but Maggie also is an unreliable source because often she says what she thinks you want to hear rather than the truth.

I am back on the old packed lunches, aren't I? Mum says it's cheaper. Dad has carved 'EAT ME' into my banana and it's made the whole banana mushy and brown, but even still it's cute. I scoff down my ham sandwiches. I play with the foil after-wards and turn it into a mini silver cat. I don't have enough foil for a tail so I pretend it was a cat that was stealing meat from the butcher's, got caught, and the butcher tried to catch him, missed him and chopped his tail off instead. I name him Barnaby.

'What's *that*?' It's Olly Supperidge. *Snorecumber*.

'What?' Oh, great. I am just WAITING for him to mention Clementine.

'That weird little attempt at foil sculpture – you getting all arts and crafty on us now, Burdock?'

I crumple the foil cat into my hand. He meows with a splat in my palm.

'So . . . that was quite something . . . that little *reading* you gave at the charity sleepover.'

'Leave it, Olly.'

'I'm being serious. It was . . . very . . . *charming*.'

My back goes up. 'Don't patronize me.'

'Fine. Don't take the compliment, but I want it for the school magazine.'

He's talking to me as he's walking away, pretending to stretch when he probs doesn't even need one. Even his walk gets me annoyed. I am surprised he even wants to talk to me after his girlfriend's stupid outburst.

I wish I could just find Leila. So that I can prove to my brain that I didn't dream her up and invent her, but also because she would know exactly what to do with the likes of Olly Supperidge.

Will is off playing football with his mates so I go along and see Mavis at Reception. I'm just going to ask her plain, clear and simples. Do you know a Leila in the school? Come on, Mavis at Reception, rack that brain of yours: DO YOU KNOW A LEILA?

'Hi, Mavis.' Mavis is eating a slice of shortbread, as per usual.

'Hello, wee girl . . .'

'I wanted to ask you something . . .'

'Fire away.'

'Do you know of a Leila?'

'In the school?'

'Yes.'

'Of course. There are three Leilas in the school. Been making friends, have you?'

I smile awkwardly. I think Mavis might be jealous. 'I'll just get them up here for you on the system.' She clicks the letters in the computer.

'She's blonde.'

'Oh no. None of these are blonde.'

Unless Mavis is deliberately trying to sabotage my plan because she wants to be my only BFF, then this is bad news.

'Can I see?'

Mavis swivels the screen round to show me, and she uses her mouse to scroll up and down. There are lots of Leilas, but the Leila I met is not one of them.

'Maybe you had too much hot chocolate and got her name confused?' Mavis tries to cheer me up.

'Maybe,' I sigh.

'That reminds me, something came for you, a lovely

girl dropped it off. I haven't seen her before, but she was in uniform. The building is so big, sometimes I forget quite how many students go here!' Mavis passes a small brown padded envelope over to me. 'I'm such a scatterbrain, there you go, it must be a fan letter or something from your fantastic reading. Now what did you want to ask me?'

'Don't worry.' The words tumble out.

I slip round the corner and hurry into the girls' toilets. The door of the girls' toilets really annoys me because the little picture is of a stick person wearing a stupid ugly triangle dress, and the boys' toilet sign is a stick person wearing trousers. It just really gets on my nervous system because girls wear trousers too and I'm sure boys like wearing dresses like my Uncle Adrian and Poppy's friend Timothy.

I, however, push open the toilet door with the stick figure wearing the triangle, even though I've NEVER worn a triangle in my life, but I think the boys' toilets smell of DISEASE, plus I'm not in the mood to see anything I shouldn't!

Inside are some olderer girls wrapping their school

shirts into belly tops by the mirror. One is plucking her eyebrows, which looks like the worst thing in the world. Why would you pull your own hairs out of their sockets? I just don't get it. This other one is scooping her hair into a big bun and pouting, and her lips look like a bulldog's bum. I enter a cubicle – I always try to go into the same one if possible – and sit on the toilet with the lid down. One of my favourite things is enjoying the graffiti on the back of the toilets; it gives me great pleasure to see that there are worserer spellerers even than what I am.

I take the small brown package. It's very light, and

on the front in black writing is writted my name. I open it up gently, and inside is a long thin box. My heart begins to race. Receiving a package like this is just so exciting. I gulp. I can hear the clatter of the other girls' voices, the squeak and bang of cubicle doors opening and shutting, the rush of the flush.

I very carefully tip the package upside down for a note, but nothing is inside. So I open the box. Inside is a posh black pen. A present from Mavis probably. *Cute.* Although it looks *very* posh, I really hope this isn't an *olive branch* type gift of approval from Olly Supperidge and this seems to have his dirty work ALL over it. I hold the pen up. It's beautiful, and then when I look closely I see something beautiful written in gold swirly writing.

Writer's Bump

Clementine is being so annoying all day, behaving like she's some kind of elevated human being, and apparently she is 'just waiting' to get *that* call from an agent to remove her out of South London and transport her to the world of Hollywood to be a superstar.

I'm thinking: Girlfriend, you *came* from America. Anyway, people aren't even saying she was good. People are saying she was TERRIBLE, and they are doing impressions of her all over the place! And that she is MEAN and they won't forget what she shouted at me during my reading, and the only reason she even got to do her song was because she burst into tears and the teachers took pity on her because she helped organize the whole event. Now I know that what I suspected is TRUE – that the entire sleepover *was* some evil ploy for her to do a concert.

The next thing I know she is walking up to me at the end of the school day, when I'm just simply actually waiting for Dad to collect me. I was just feeling sorry for myself because Will had football after school. To be honest, I wish I'd just walked. My pen is gripped tightly in my hand.

'Darcy . . .' Clementine says, all smug, oh great, shove off. 'I just wanted to say, well *done* for having a stab at the performance the other night. I did feel a bit guilty for heckling during your reading, but I was just putting you through your paces, as that kind of stuff happens in the real world. You can obviously take the heat. I am so *proud* of you for being so brave.'

OH, SHUT UP, what a lying weasel. She is SO fake.

'*And* it was great to share a stage with you. I'm sure it made you feel so professional. I am just so glad it wasn't a competition because that might have made it a really tricky reading for you, but anyway . . .'

Just as her face is about to melt into a jar of preserved patronize jam, guess who flounces up to the school gate to meet me?

My Uncle Adrian.

He is wearing an Adidas tracksuit, false eyelashes, glitter on his cheeks and Minnie Mouse ears on his head.

'What's up, babes?' Uncle Adrian pulls me in for a tight hug. He is holding a bag of warm sugary doughnuts from the bakery.

Clementine wants to die. She is amazed. HA!

'Hi, I'm Clementine.' She flicks her hair and smiles all white-teethed and broad, her lips all shiny like the shiny yolk of a fried egg.

'Oh, the singer?' Uncle Adrian laughs.

'That's right, yes.' Clementine giggles and wraps her arms around me as if we are BFFs. 'Did Darcy tell you about me?'

'She sure did.' The glitter on Uncle Adrian's skin twinkles. It's beautiful. I am nervous a bit in case these two become best mates. Not that they ever would, but sometimes Uncle Adrian is magnetized towards crazy divas and scary evil people because he finds them hilarious. But I am the most importantest person in his life and I DON'T think he would ever want to magnetize towards her . . . but I hadn't told him the horrible things she had shouted during the show because I knew he would lose his mind.

'Awww, Darcy is *so* cute,' Clementine gushes. 'You know we went to primary school together, oh, we go way back, her best friend Will used to have *such* a crush on me, so cute.' Adrian is *pretending* to look interested.

'I am actually a singer,' she adds, 'well, and actress, model, campaigner. I actually performed . . . at the sleepover?'

'Oh yes, I heard.' Uncle Adrian smiled.

'Awwwwwwwww, you did? Oh, Darcy, you're such a doll. What did she say?'

'Oh, she didn't say anything, she didn't have to. I can just tell it would have been hideous. Because you are. Hideous.'

WHAT? My jaw drops.

Clementine giggles nervously. 'Pardon me?'

'You heard. You are a brat. A shiny, ugly brat with weird plastic lips and ridiculous fake hair to match your plastic, ridiculous, fake personality.'

'I don't believe this . . .' Clementine stutters. 'Excuse me, you don't know me, who even are you?' she spits, hands on hips. I've never seen her so speechless.

'I'm Uncle Adrian.' He beams the flashiest smile ever, then he links my arm. 'Come on, Darcy, these doughnuts won't eat themselves.'

And I am shaking. Unable to look up but

completely able to hear Clementine's screams raging after us as we walk away.

'My father will sue you!' she barks. 'You won't get away with this! Soon I'll be famous and you'll be sorry!'

And I am so proud. My Uncle Adrian.

That's right.

'Nothing's up . . .' I say, picking at the sugar round the outside, not really sure if actually I like doughnut or just the sugar and jam bit. Really it's just deep-fried blistered bread roll, which is a bit weird when you think about it. Can I tell Adrian all about Leila? Yes, I suppose I can. So I do.

When I've finished telling him he reaches for another doughnut. 'My diet starts tomorrow,' he says out of the corner of his mouth. I nod in pretend belief. 'So remind me why you were running around the school in the night anyway?'

I feel nervous. Yes, Uncle Adrian isn't my dad, but he also is a growed up that could judge me and have private angry thoughts towards me, but also he is my uncle and does love me.

'Can you keep a secret?'

'Not really.' He cracks up. 'But I'm willing to try.'

'Leila wanted to steal back her confiscated bow and arrows.'

'Amazing! A bow and arrows? Who is she like – Robin Hood? That terrific redhead from *Brave*?' Uncle Adrian sniggers and shakes his head, 'I mean . . . let me try and be responsible for like five seconds . . . OK, that's naughty, did you help her?'

I try not to laugh at Uncle Adrian trying to sound stern, but also I a bit want to be told off because it feels good to get this private escapade of weirdness off my shoulders. 'Yes, kind of, that's why I read the story.'

'In front of the entire school?'

'Yes.'

'So you read a story that you wrote in front of the entire school, risking your whole social status, just so a girl – who you had NEVER even spoken to before – could steal back her confiscated bow and arrows?'

Gosh, it really does sound even crazier out loud and coming out of the mouth of somebody else. 'Errr . . . yes?'

'Girlfriend, you crazy!' Uncle Adrian puts his hand forward for another doughnut. 'Too much?'

'I won't tell if you don't.'

'Deal.' Uncle Adrian shakes hands with me and lifts his third doughnut out of the packet. 'And so, since then you've not seen her, not heard from her, nothing?'

'Well, she left this for me.' I show Uncle Adrian the pen.

'What a lovely gift,' he smiles, but he holds it weirdly as his fingers are mostly sprinkled in sugar crystals and grease.

'I know. But she left it at Reception and Mavis says she doesn't even recognize her really, but that's easily understandable because the school is so big and there are so many students.'

'You could always print out the story that you wrote for her – you know, the fossil dragon drama – because she didn't get a chance to hear it, did she, when you read it at the sleepover?'

'No, that's when she was . . .' I get nervous talking about naughty bad things in front of Uncle Adrian.

'Stealing back her stolen bow and arrows?'

'Yeah,' I admit, but he doesn't get cross.

'So, address the story to her in an envelope and leave it with Mavis at Reception, use her as a postman, and tell Mavis that when Leila comes to collect it to ask her who she is, what class she's in, etc.'

'What a good idea!'

'I know. Thank you. Tea?'

'I'll make it.'

And as I head downstairs I am just replaying over and over what Uncle Adrian said to Clementine and not even believing it's true and feeling so haps about it.

Chapter Sixteen

'She still hasn't come by for it, Darcy. I'm sorry.' Mavis shakes her head, really knows how to *feel* my disappointment. I had printed the story out just like how Uncle Adrian and I discussed and it took me ages to type up and get all the words all perfect. I put it in a lovely envelope and writted *Leila* on the front in my ideal best handwriting.

'I don't understand.'

'I will ask around in the staffroom today. I'll put some effort into it, but I assure you, she is a total mystery.'

'OK. But I don't get it – it's been there for *ages* now.' I look at my envelope. It's all THERE and not moving. 'Maybe she came and you missed her, Mavis?'

I ask her. 'Didn't she want to come by and see if I got my package?'

'Not to my knowledge.' Mavis pretends to ruffle through some papers in case she missed something that she KNOWS wasn't there. 'And you know me, unless Darcy Burdock is reading a story in the main hall, I don't leave this little desk.'

'I know.' I get a bit Angrosaurus-rex with Mavis, even though it isn't her fault, but there is nobody else to blame.

'Just leave it a couple more days.'

'I want to take it back.' I get angry. I am angry at Leila for making me wish to be her friend and then dumping me like that, and the fact that the envelope just sits there like an evil reminder hurts me even more each day.

'No, hen, leave it a little longer.'

'Can I just have it back again, please?'

'Why not wait and see?' Mavis tries with me. She still has hope, poor ignorant Mavis.

'I've waited and seed long enough.' I take the envelope with my dragon story inside, and do it in a real hurry because I can feel a flush of embarrass-ment coming on quick as can be.

At home is major depressing. I start to think that perhaps I am prematurely evolving into a teenager because the world isn't on my side. Adrian is leaving tomorrow to go back to New York because he has to go back to work. This makes me more than sad because it's so nice having him here; it's like always having a big brother around. Mum is annoying me because every second word is all dumb and stupid and annoying and about money, and Hector isn't helping because he's going through the 'why' phase, which means when every question is why . . . obviously, and so a conversation with Mum looks a lot like this:

    'WHY can't I have a new toy?'

    'Because you can't.'

    'WHY?'

    'Because I said so.'

    'WHY?'

    'Because we don't have the money.'

'WHY?'

'Because we don't.'

'WHY?'

A moment's silence and then he will start again.

'But I thought Dad was going to work at a toy shop.'

'That wasn't certain.'

'WHY?'

'Because it isn't.'

'WHY?'

'Because he hasn't heard from the toy shop owners yet.'

'WHY?'

'Because these things can take a while.'

'WHY?'

'I don't know.'

'WHY?'

'SHUT UP!'

I don't know if you've seen the film *Mary Poppins,* but in the film there's this family called the Bankses who aren't getting along very well. They aren't getting along because Mr Banks has heaps of work to do and sometimes he forgets to let the children be children because he is so bogged down with normal-ish things like paperwork and money. One day Mary Poppins arrives – she comes down from the sky with an umbrella with a talking parrot at the end, and she carries a big carpet suitcase and inside are things that are WAY too big for a normal suitcase, like a lamp and stuff. Mary Poppins makes the Bankses' home special, and all cheered up by her magical love for life and little tricks and snags that make life a bit easier. I love it. Uncle Adrian is my Mary Poppins.

Adrian sharpens his scissors and sits Hector down in the chair first. Hector is nervous and cries a bit.

'Does it hurt to chop hair off?' he moans.

'Course not, it's like cutting your nails.'

'I hate it when you trim my claws down,' he moans.

'Hector, look . . .' Poppy knows what to do. It isn't hard to make him sit still, because he loves watching videos of himself off one of our phones. Poppy shows him a clip of him rolling Pork into a duvet, another one of him eating cereal and another of him tumbling down the staircase in a guitar case. He is obsessed with looking at *his* own self.

Adrian deals with them tangly curls in five minutes flat. Next Poppy sits down in the chair. Mum usually chops Poppy's hair, a good haircut, a perfect little tidy bob. Adrian tidies it up and compliments her, un-surprisingly, on the 'shine' of her hair. *Snore*.

Dad sits down next and gets a simple trim. He keeps saying to Uncle Adrian, 'That'll do, mate. That'll do.' But Uncle Adrian just quietly ignores him and continues to snip until Dad relaxes. Adrian even trims Dad's beard too, which Dad complains is now all itchy.

I sit down after Dad. The chair is all hot and both-ered from everyone's individual bums. Adrian quickly pecks away at my curls, knots and tangles. Adrian knows better than to comment on my knots because I'll simply throw a tantrum thunderstorm.

Lastly, Mum sits down in the chair. My mum moans forty hundred times about the haircut. She hasn't had one in approximately one thousand and five years because she thinks it's a waste of money. Then she says that there is washing to be done and *blah blah blah*, but before you know it her hair is getting all chopped off and falling to the floor like clumps of guinea-pig tail. Adrian spends the mostly time on her, perfecting all the corners, and tiny snips of triangle shark-fin shreds of Mum's locks scatter on the kitchen tiles. Adrian's eyes are very focused, and eventually Mum closes her eyes, her arms flop down by her side and we all go very quiet.

'Done.' Uncle Adrian says, and Dad turns round from his coffee making and nearly smashes the cup to the ground – Mum looks so beautiful extreme.

'Mollie,' Dad whooshes out in a love breath, 'you look stunning.'

'Oh, shut up, don't be silly,' Mum laughs off, and begins to dust the hairs off her chest.

'You do look MEGA!' Uncle Adrian keeps touching the hair, he won't leave it alone. 'Gosh, sometimes I just want to lock myself in jail, it's got to be a crime to be THIS good a hairdresser!' We all laugh at him as

he screwfaces
himself in
the mirror.
'I am so good at
doing hair it's a
tragedy,' he adds. 'I
HATE myself.' He
fans his face. He's so
funny.

But in all serious-
ness Mum does look
utterly wonderful.
Poppy is already trying to tie
various hairbands and bows into
Mum's hair but she needs nothing.
She is perfect as she is.

'You should take Mummy out for
a date.' Poppy grips onto Dad's leg.

'Yes, I think I should do.' Dad smiles.

'No, don't be silly, I've got the chicken defrosting,
we can't afford it.' Mum brushes her new hair behind
her ear, all shy, but she looks so dazzling.

'Don't be ridiculous, of course we can.'

'No, that's not what our savings are for.'

'Mollie, that's *exactly* what our savings are for.'

Mum looks all shyly.

'I'll babysit . . . or lunatic-sit . . . whichever is easiest,' says Uncle Adrian.

And that makes us all so pleased and happy becaused we get one whole Uncle Adrian to our own selves, which probs means something disgusting and greasy and wonderful for dinner, and plus he knows all the best films which even have bad words in them! *Hooray!*

Mum is in a good lovely mood. She has litted candles all in the bathroom and run the bath to the top, but she does not flood it because she is not a fruit-cake like me. I LOVE cake. But not *fruitcake* because it tastes like goned-off fruit, and once it's in your tummy it tries to poison you with heaviness. It's like eating a brick of raisins. Mum has bubbles, the posh purple ones that come in the glass jar with the ribbon and the posh stopper that we're not allowed to touch. She doesn't let us even come in the bathroom to talk to her, which annoys me because it's the only time I get a good decent chance to even have a good old chinwag with Mum, but she just keeps on humming a song I don't know and has the door shutted. If one of us knocks and says, 'Mum, can we come in?' she says, 'I just want some peace and quiet.'

And so we have to just say this: 'Oh.'

Next Mum comes out of the bathroom and leaves the bathroom in a hot wash of bubbles and lavender-smelling steam; her new hair is all pinned up and dry though. She looks like the women in the ice cream adverts a lot. In Mum and Dad's bedroom, she keeps humming and I think about sitting on the bed with Poppy and helping her choose her dress, but I think that perhaps instead we should just let her have some privacy.

Poppy and I sit outside their room for a bit and we can hear the clattering of make-up and the swishes of hangers on the clothes rail. We can hear Dad's posh fancy shoes scuffing on the hallway floor downstairs where he willed obviously be looking identical to Prince Charming. We watch him over the banister at the top of the stairs where he can't see us.

Poppy slumps her head into her hands. 'I think I'm sad.'

'Why?'

'I thought I was going to marry Dad. Now Dad's taking Mum out for a date, and not you and not me.'

'You can't marry Dad, Poppy, he's your dad.'

'Yes, but he's the only man I truly love.'

'Yes, but I think it's a different kind of love.'

'I don't, I think it's a really trickly situation. I can't even marry Hector because he's too young . . . Oh, I suppose I *could* marry Uncle Adrian!' she suddenly yelps up, elated. 'Unless he plans to marry that white cat he lives with.'

'I don't think he'll marry the cat, Poppy,' I reassure her.

'Let's hope not,' she adds.

You have to love your family, don't you? You don't get a choice. It's a decision invented before you were even born. Mum and Dad married up because they loved each other and they weren't *even* family. It wasn't an *order* to love each other. It was a non-compulsory romantic type of love. One I will never get my head around. A fairy-tale love, I guess. One that is GROSS if you ask me, but we have to put up with it. And even though it's yucky seeing them be all kissy and mushy, they don't do it very often.

At last, the door to Mum and Dad's bedroom creaks open and Mum comes out in a droplet rainy haze of that perfume I love and hairspray that gently floats through the air like a lemonade bubble cloud.

Mum has on a beautiful long orange dress and one bajillion lovely bangles and bracelets.

Her hair is all down and bouncy, her make-up is quite a magazine look and she has on pink lipstick. And then a tall pair of clippy-cloppy shoes.

Poppy and I both drop our jaws to the ground, and Mum steps past us sooooo confidently and begins to trot down the stairs, slightly wibbly in her heels but just looking like a parrot swan.

'I think I actually just want to marry Mum,' Poppy gushes.

'Me too.' I nod.

We completely, obviously, because we are dinosaur children from the worst part of the earth, ruin the moment that Dad claps eyes on Mum all made up, because we are all jumpy and over-excited and ruin it all so terribly, and Uncle Adrian knows to just shove Mum and Dad into a taxi before we explode from showy-off excitement. We wave them off from the window; Hector gets carried away and presses his bare bum up against the glass. *Who even gets that excited about two people, that ARE NOT YOU, going for dinner?*

Timothy, Poppy's best mate, and Will both get to come over for a bit as they are completely desperado to meet Uncle Adrian in the flesh as they've hearded just so much about him.

'Oh, fantastic, you've come on your BMX.' Uncle Adrian checks out Will's *ride*.

'Yeah, I ride it everywhere – you into bikes then?' Will stands proudly.

'No. It just means you can pick the fried chicken up from the shop.'

Will cracks up with laughter. 'No worries,' he grins.

'I'll go with you, Will,' I smile.

'In that case, get double the chicken. And cans of fizzy drink. And not diet ones.'

It's a warm evening, with the clouds turning into pink and the fierce orange ball of sun still trying to get the chance to meet the moon. Now that's a love that will rarely be able to happen – the sun and the moon will never properly be in love. The precious chicken cargo sits on Will's handlebars, balanced side by side, and the wheels go round.

At home we eat chicken like we've never even eated before, and with Uncle Adrian around you have to eat so quick because he finishes his food so fast and then starts taking it off your own plate. Uncle Adrian should actually be a really mahoosive chubby person, but somehow he isn't. Uncle Adrian is also so slyed, because he keeps picking the fried skin off all our chicken, leaving us with that ugly grey bit inside that you don't want to actually *see*. This is the greatest take-away because it comes with baked beans. If only *every* takeaway camed with baked beans.

Then is the best bit. Uncle Adrian brings in a bag of Granny's old clothes. He had collected it when he went to get her belongings. It's full to the brim of amazing Granny wonderful junk: big jumpers, tights, old wilty floral dresses, shoes, knitted cardigans, pearls, beads, glasses, and we all dress up and then do a Granny catwalk, even though we are soooo stuffed. We all get the giggles so hard we can't breathe. Then I re-enact what Uncle Adrian said to Clementine about 189734560 times, and we laugh until our ribs almost snap.

When we get our breaths back we have tea and watch *E.T.*, this excellent film about an alien that comes to earth and becomes best friends with a boy called Elliott, and they eat Skittles and at the end Elliott rides his bicycle really fast, and then before you know it, it leaps up high into the sky and even over the moon. I cried in it. So did Uncle Adrian. So did Poppy. And Timothy. But not Will, because he was a tough cookie, and not Hector because he was asleep.

And later on, after when Will and Timothy have

gonned home and we are all in bed for ages, I hear the key in the front door and Mum and Dad tumble in, giggling and stomping about, and it's *very* late and I should have been asleep but I have a huge smile swept over my mouth.

Chapter Seventeen

I don't really want to talk about when Uncle Adrian left the next day, because it was so sad that it made me angry. Poppy didn't want to even look at him she was so livid herself. We all clung to him, letting boiling hot tears dribble down our cheeks.

'My cat needs feeding,' he kept saying as his excuse, but really we knew he had a life back in New York and he wanted to cry a bit too. He tried to make a few jokes, calling us 'lunatics' and 'hooligans' and 'drama queens' and 'the reason I live', then a tear sneakily droplets from his eye too. 'I'll be back,' he sniffles into us, and then he says, 'I promise.'

And we know it's one he will keep.

Once Adrian gets drived away by the taxi we all frump down onto the sofa. Granny-less. Pork-less. Adrian-less. Money-less. Mum looks a bit teary. She is the one who we need to all look after. We all hug her close. We are so sad for her. We love our mum so much. She is the most special woman on the entire planet and ALL the other planets too, and if I ever losted her then I would want to lose me.

'We love you, Mum,' we all take turns to say.

'I can't believe it, my mum has actually gone,' she sniffs. 'She's buried, in the ground.'

'Want me to dig her up for you?' Hector asks, and we all try really hard not to laugh as his face is so deadpan serious. 'I'm not joking, I've got really good at digging.'

When we get our breaths back, the phone rings. 'I'll get it.' Dad leaps up. 'It's only going to be bad news.' He winks at us – it's our running joke these days, because every time the phone rings it is mostly bad news.

Mum turns to me. 'Your poem at the funeral was

really special, Darcy. I am so pleased you read it out, it made me so proud.'

'Yes, it was AMMMMMMAZZZZZINNGGGG.' Poppy clicks her finger. 'Uh-huh, honey.'

'Have you got another story you could read us? I'm in the mood for one.'

I think. I have got some . . . but not in neat writing and sometimes I stumble over the words and find it hard to read . . . wait . . . I do have the one typed up all neat and tidy that was meant for Leila. In the envelope. The dragon story. I could read that.

'Yes, I do actually, let me just get it.'

In my room, I open up the envelope and out falls the story, and then a note flies out.

It's written in swirly handwriting and it says:

I saw this in Mavis's office — she didn't even see me take it or replace it.

So let's keep it that way.

You'll have to give me a new story. I heard this one already. I didn't get my bow back — I couldn't miss hearing your story. I watched you read to the entire school the way you did, and it was one of the bravest things I've ever seen. That Clementine will get what's good for her . . . TRUST ME! Revenge is a dish best served defrosted. I know in your brain you think the dragon from your story is me and you are Saskia, but YOU are the dragon.

And btw there's no point trying to find me, my name isn't even really Leila!

I hold the story close to my chest and as tight as humanly possible for the possibility of finding my new friend.

I charge downstairs with the story in hand, ready to read. Ready for change.

'Ready?' I beam as I bounce into the living room. My whole family looks back at me like they've been hitted by a bus.

'What's happened?' I ask.

'Dad's just been offered a huge job, all of the carpentry and flooring of a brand new multi-storey toy shop! A full renovation! It's a big contract! They want to sign right away!' Mum winks at us because we weren't meant to know, REMEMBER!

My dad leaps in the air, squeezing us all together. 'We're saved! We're saved! It's all OK! It's all OK!'

'So . . .' I say to Mavis over tea and shortbread at lunch time. 'What does your actual job entail?' I ask her.

'You're not thinking of becoming a receptionist, are you, Darcy? You must be a writer!'

'As a backup plan,' I reply.

'OK, it's paperwork, filing, answering the phone, boring work. A donkey could do it.'

I giggle. 'Do you like it?'

'I like this part of it, tea and biscuits.'

'Do you . . . ever . . . confiscate things?' I'm getting warmer . . .

'Not really, I'm not a meanie like that, but sometimes if another teacher confiscates something they might bring it to me to hide or return.'

ZOOOOOOOP.

'Really?' I play along. 'And where do you keep it?'

'Oh, in that cupboard, just there?'

'What's the strangest most peculiar thing you've EVER had in your confiscated cupboard?'

'Oh, I don't know . . . I guess once I had a blow-up palm tree . . . that was weird. It popped. It was actually quite heart-breaking. I liked it.'

'Anything else?' I ask.

'I don't know . . . you writers, always on the hunt for inspiration, aren't you? I'm hoping you're going to write something about me one day!' she shrills and winks at me. 'You're so nosy!' THAT'S RICH! I think, but I have to keep her sweet if I am going to get closer to locating Leila's bow.

'Yeah, objects can be very inspiring.'

'Go and have a look,' she says. 'I'm sure it's a load of old rubbish.'

YES!

I walk over to the cupboard, open it up. It's full of little labelled boxes of balls, skipping ropes, books, computer games, hairbrushes, headphones, mobile phones and then, right there at the back . . .

The bow.

'Wow!' I reach for the bow. 'Who does this belong

to?' I can't believe it . . . I can't believe it . . . I am about to find out her actual name . . .

'Oh, what's her name now?' Mavis has a look in her little record book, shows me the name and I smile.

Agatha Leila Thingling.

Leila is her *middle* name! No wonder Mavis couldn't find her on the system.

Agatha. Leila. Thingling. And just to think she had the audacity to laugh at MY name!

HA!

'That's been there a while now,' Mavis tuts. 'Who brings a bow and arrows to school? Ridiculous.'

I know who.

'Mavis, perhaps we should get all these confiscated items back to their owners?'

'Ooh, I don't know. I haven't got the time, pet.'

'I can help you,' I say.

Mavis looks at me, her head slanted. I quickly have to look less keen.

'I honestly don't mind. I mean, I know it's my lunch break, but at least I can spend more time with you?' That should melt her heart.

'Yes, OK. Why not.'

'Let's start with this bow. It belongs to Agatha Leila Thingling . . . never heard of her before,' I add. 'Have you?'

Chapter Eighteen

Dear Grandma,

I am sure you heard. Granny died. I'm sure you're well happy about that, because now it's undeniable that we love you the best because we have no choice. You can't be compared. So feel free at this stage to turn evil and become a nasty wretched wicked witch. We won't have a choice, you will still remain our best grandma.

At first I didn't know how to react when she died because I didn't really think I loved her much because I didn't really know her. Not like how I know or love you anyway.

But then seeing Mum sad made me more sad, and also she did adopt my mum and that's quite a wonderful thing. And my mum is quite wonderful anyway.

So this is really just a warning, mostly to say I don't think you should stay in our house, because it seems to kill old people unexpectedly, but also really to say how much we love you. Which we never say enough. I hope I'm not too late and you're not already dead. You're getting on, old dear, bless you, I would hate for you to just one day croak on us.

Also I've taken the trouble of this list of why you're a better grandma, for your own feedback, see it like a review. As you can see for yourself, you pretty much tick every box and smash it all round, so well done for that.

I hope you don't never die, I would seriously hate that.

Darcy x

I push the letter into the post box and then skedaddle

into the car after my family. Dad is driving and reverses into the road. We wind through the city, watching the world flutter past our windows. The radio is singing our favourite songs as if we personally picked the playlist. We pull up at a big building. It's giant, actually. There is scaffolding covering it so you can't really make out much. People wearing hard hats are carrying poles, drinking tea, drilling and hammering.

'What's this?' Hector asks.

'For now it's a derelict old building, but in about six months this is going to be a toy shop.'

'OH, WOW!' Poppy rubs her eyes dramatically, Hector looks confused and I bite my lip, my head already spinning with ideas.

'Shall we go and have a look?' Dad asks, and he picks Hector up. Poppy links his arm, I hold Poppy's other hand and Dad puts his arm around Mum.

'Darcy . . .' Dad says. 'Uncle Adrian told me about your story. With Saskia and the museum where she wants to help her dad. I loved the idea of the dragon. Your inspiration inspired me and I want to show you the design plans for the toy shop.'

He unveils a big scroll of paper. It's hard to see what's what because it's all professional lines and arrows, colours and codes that make no sense to me. And then scribbled on top, in Dad's whirling sprawling freehand drawing skills, are loads of dragons. Dad beams, and he squeezes my shoulder.

'It's going to be dragon-themed, the entire toy shop. Each floor a different dragon, the banister of the stairs is going to be a long dragon's tail and the lift is going to be dragon wings. It's a big job, but the clients love the idea. And so do I.'

'And so do I.' I nearly cry with so much unbelievable pride.

'And I,' Mum sniffs, nearly crying.

'And me,' Poppy says.

And we wait for Hector to say the same too, but he is already running fast ahead, his coat catching the wind as he races into the doors of the new shop.

Our new future.

And it looks like he has wings.

Acknowledgements

Thank you to 'Team Darcy' at Penguin Random House. You are all amazing. A big thank you to Natalie Doherty for doing an amazing editorial job on the book, for allowing me to write honestly and truthfully and for your continued support. I have loved working with you so much. Thank you to Will Steele for the design of the book. We put the illustrations of the pages together over the Christmas break, emailing back and forth with twiglet-dust-powdered fingertips. Thanks again. Thank you to Andrea MacDonald and Annie Eaton for your encouragement and love for the books. Lauren Hyett, Harriet Venn and Alex Taylor for blazing the Darcy trail. And of course Sue, for her copyedit and making it look clean and tidy.

Thank you to my agents at United Agents, Jodie Hodges, Jane Willis, Julian Dickson, Dan Usztan and Emily Talbot.

Thank you to Cathryn Summerhayes and Becky Thomas.

Thank you to all the bookshops and sellers, libraries and librarians, blogs and bloggers, schools and individuals that have pushed and supported Darcy. You know who you are. I am grateful.

Thank you to my family and friends. Daisy and Hector, the whole series basically belongs to the both of you. Idiots. I am obsessed with you.

And Pig the pug. You were there too. I guess.

And finally, thank you to my readers. This is the fourth Darcy Burdock book in the series and I have already started writing the fifth. Writing her is an absolute pleasure, because I can't wait to show you lot. Thanks for sticking around.

Love Laura x